THE
SPRITE
SISTERS

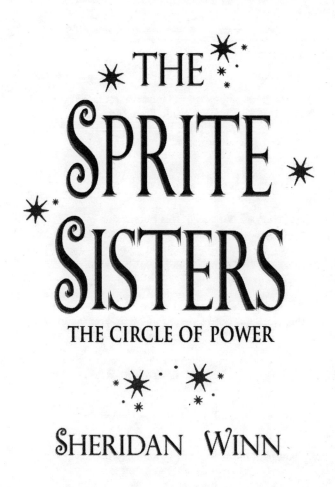

THE SPRITE SISTERS

THE CIRCLE OF POWER

SHERIDAN WINN

PICCADILLY PRESS • LONDON

First published in Great Britain in 2008
by Piccadilly Press Ltd,
5 Castle Road, London NW1 8PR
www.piccadillypress.co.uk

A catalogue record for this book is available
from the British Library.

ISBN: 978 1 85340 963 9

Printed and bound in Great Britain by CPI Bookmarque, Croydon
Cover design by Simon Davis
Cover illustration by Anna Gould
Sprite Towers map by Chris Winn

Mixed Sources
Product group from well-managed
forests and other controlled sources
www.fsc.org Cert no. TT-COC-002227
© 1996 Forest Stewardship Council
FSC

*For my parents,
Alan & Janet Ebbage,
with love and thanks*

And in memory of Littlewood House

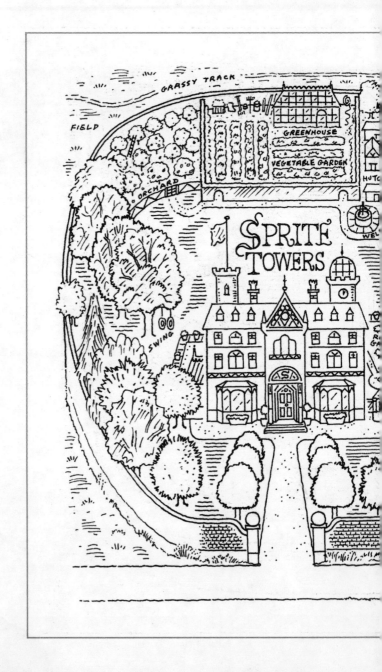

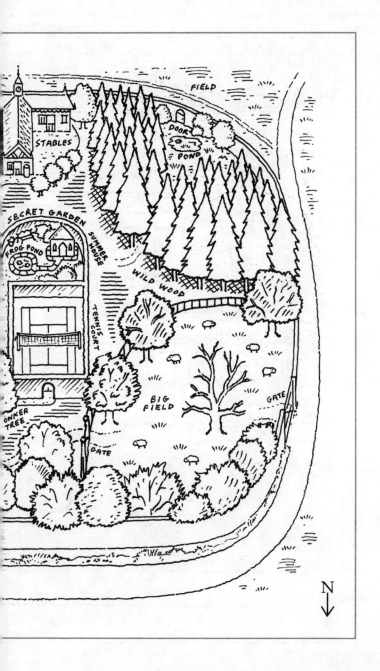

THE CIRCLE
OF POWER

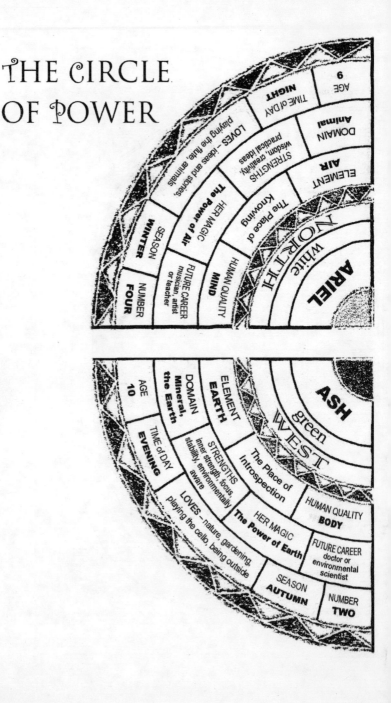

AGE **6**

TIME of DAY **NIGHT**

DOMAIN **Animal**

ELEMENT **AIR**

LOVES - ideas and stories, playing the flute, animals

STRENGTHS wisdom, creativity, practical ideas

The Place of Knowing

HER MAGIC **The Power of Air**

HUMAN QUALITY **MIND**

FUTURE CAREER musician, artist or teacher

SEASON **WINTER**

NUMBER **FOUR**

ARIEL

NORTH White

AGE **10**

TIME of DAY **EVENING**

DOMAIN **Mineral, the Earth**

ELEMENT **EARTH**

STRENGTHS inner strength, focus stability, environmentally aware

The Place of Introspection

LOVES - nature, gardening, playing the cello, being outside

HER MAGIC **The Power of Earth**

HUMAN QUALITY **BODY**

FUTURE CAREER doctor or environmental scientist

SEASON **AUTUMN**

NUMBER **TWO**

ASH

WEST green

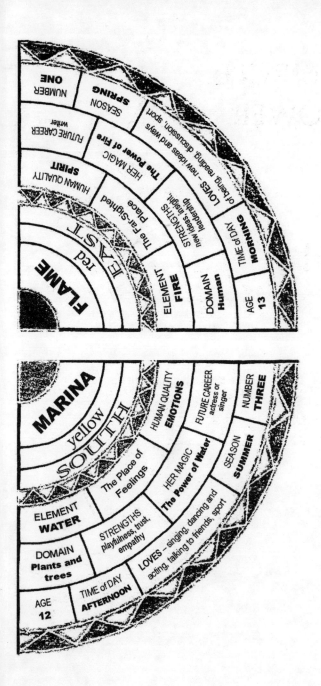

FLAME red **EAST**

NUMBER ONE

SEASON SPRING

FUTURE CAREER writer

HER MAGIC The Power of Fire

HUMAN QUALITY SPIRIT

STRENGTHS leadership, new ideas, insight

LOVES – new ideas and ways of being, reading, discussion, sport

The Far-Sighted Place

ELEMENT FIRE

DOMAIN Human

TIME of DAY MORNING

AGE 13

MARINA yellow **SOUTH**

HUMAN QUALITY EMOTIONS

FUTURE CAREER actress or singer

NUMBER THREE

The Place of Feelings

HER MAGIC The Power of Water

SEASON SUMMER

ELEMENT WATER

STRENGTHS playfulness, trust, empathy

LOVES – singing, dancing and acting, talking to friends, sport

DOMAIN Plants and trees

AGE 12

TIME of DAY AFTERNOON

CHAPTER ONE

ARIEL FINDS HER POWER

FLAME SPRITE kicked off her bright red sheet and stretched out her legs. She pushed back her thick, copper-coloured hair from her face, opened her left eye and kept her right eye closed: she wanted to wake up slowly. In front of her something purple blazed. She opened her right eye and focused: it was her new bra.

Flame, eldest of the Sprite Sisters and thirteen years old yesterday, had just started wearing a bra. There it was, hanging from the back of the chair beside her bed – a bright purple lacy bra with padded cups and fluorescent pink piping.

Funny things, bras, she thought, and screwed up her nose.

1

She closed her eyes again and enjoyed the softness of her bed. The fresh smell of a summer morning wafted through the open window. She felt the warmth of the air on her face and could hear birds singing outside in the garden.

It was Sunday the tenth of June. Yesterday, she and her sister Ariel had their birthdays and a joint party – a disco in the huge dining room of Sprite Towers. It had been one of the best days of Flame's life. They had all danced for hours – she had danced with Quinn – the coloured lights flashing on the high ceiling and the DJ bouncing about behind his decks.

Sprite Towers had been lit up and alive. People had walked from room to lofty room, smiling and laughing. Outside, the garden had looked magical: Mum and Dad had hung hundreds of silvery-white lights in the trees and bushes. The seventy guests and family had eaten a delicious barbecue, sitting on rugs on the lawn. Then there'd been the disco. They'd had such fun.

Flame held out her long hands and looked at her fingers. They tingled and grew hot. She smiled.

There is a lot of power in these hands, she thought.

Along the corridor, high up on the second floor of Sprite Towers, Ariel, the youngest of the Sprite Sisters, lay against her pillows. She loved her bedroom, with its sugar-pink walls and dove-grey carpet and the way the sun streamed through the window in the morning. She was thinking about the party the evening before. She was happy.

Nine! She was nine years old!

Oh – there it was again, this strange tingling in her fingers. She had felt it the day before.

Ariel held up her hands and looked at them: they were soft, pink and dimply on the back, as usual. She turned them over and looked at the tiny lines that ran across her palms. The tingly sensation started again.

Her fingers felt all hot and wiggly.

Ariel looked at her right index finger and pointed it at the line of six small furry teddy bears that sat on the shelf near her bed.

She had the strangest idea – and raised her finger ever so slightly.

The teddy bears lifted in the air and hovered, a few centimetres off the shelf. When she moved her finger down, the teddy bears plopped back on to the shelf.

This is very strange, thought Ariel. Her teddy bears had moved!

She looked at her finger again: it appeared to be the same pink, stubby finger as it was yesterday.

She looked around the room. Everything seemed the same.

She pointed her finger and raised it: again, the teddy bears hovered in the air. When she lowered it, they plopped down on to the shelf.

Ariel raised her finger a third time, and this time wiggled it about: the teddy bears rose up off the shelf and hovered in the air – wiggling.

Then she pointed her hot, tingly finger at a book lying on the floor beside her bed. It began to rise up in the air. She pulled her finger towards her and the book moved towards her, in mid-air. Then she lowered her finger and the book dropped gently on to her bed.

She did it again – lifted the book from the bed, but this time quickly pulled her finger away. The book banged down on the carpet.

Ariel Sprite clapped her hands with delight and decided she must tell her sisters.

'Are you awake?' called Ariel, as she opened the door of Flame's bedroom. She walked over the dark navy-blue carpet past neat shelves of books.

'Hmm . . . just,' yawned Flame. 'What's up?'

'I've got a secret to tell you,' said Ariel, climbing into bed beside her.

Flame smiled and sat up. She knew what her little sister was about to say.

Ariel waved her hands in the air as she demonstrated how she had made her teddy bears and book rise into the air.

The laughter in Flame's room woke Marina and Ash. They

came in to see what was happening and sat down on the bright red bed.

'I've got a magic trick!' said Ariel, in her breathy voice. 'Watch!'

She pointed her finger at Flame's purple bra. It lifted off the chair and hovered in the air. Marina and Ash laughed.

'Put it down!' said Flame, her green eyes flashing. She was very touchy about the bra.

Ariel lowered her finger and the bra dropped back on to the chair.

'Isn't it funny?' she said.

The girls smiled at their pretty little sister with her soft blond hair, huge grey eyes and ski-jump nose.

Ariel looked at her finger. 'It feels all tingly,' she said.

For a few seconds, her older sisters watched her in silence.

Then Flame said, 'Ariel, there is something we need to tell you.'

'What?' asked Ariel.

'You have a magical power,' said Flame. 'We Sprite Sisters all do.'

'What – you mean you can do this too?' asked Ariel.

'Not quite that, but something similar, yes,' nodded Flame.

'Oh,' said Ariel. 'So I'm not the only one?'

'No, sugar plum.' Marina shook her head and smiled her wide smile.

'I thought I'd finally found something you lot couldn't

5

do.' Ariel pushed out her bottom lip and rested her chin in the cup of her hand.

Marina laughed. 'There are lots of things you can do that we can't do, but magic isn't one of them!'

'Well, what tricks can you do?' challenged Ariel, raising her chin.

Marina opened her mouth to start to answer, but Flame interrupted.

'Each of our powers is based on one of the four elements,' said Flame.

'Why do you always do that?' said Marina, tossing back her dark, curly hair.

'Do what?' asked Flame.

'Butt in when I'm just about to say something!'

'I was going to explain to Ariel about our powers,' said Flame. 'SORRY!'

For a moment there was silence as Flame and Marina, only a year apart in age, glared at one another.

'Oh, stop it!' said Ariel. 'What's an element?'

'The four elements that make up the world are Fire, Water, Earth and Air,' said Flame. 'Our powers are each based on one of those elements. My power harnesses the element of Fire: I can burn and melt things or illuminate them. I can make bolts of lightning and light up a room – but that's because I'm thirteen now and my powers have grown stronger.'

'Wow!' blinked Ariel.

'I work with the element of Water,' said Marina.

'Is that because you have blue eyes?' asked Ariel.

'It might be,' replied Marina. 'But my magic power means I can control anything fluid and can feel if there is anything fluid around. I can do things like create a huge river, or make ice, or dry up all the water in something so there's none left.'

Ariel blinked again and her mouth dropped open.

'And I work with the element of Earth,' said Ash.

'I expect that's why you like growing things in the garden,' said Ariel.

'I'm sure you're right.' Ash smiled her quiet smile. 'My power allows me to do things like make holes in the ground to swallow things up, or make things grow roots like a tree, so they can't move. I can find hidden objects by moving my hands over surfaces and feeling what's underneath.'

Ariel stared at Ash in amazement.

'Close your mouth – you look like a goldfish!' said Marina, pushing up Ariel's chin.

'If we stood on the four points of the compass, I would stand at the East, which represents Fire,' continued Flame. 'Marina would stand at the South, which is the position for Water; Ash at the West represents Earth; and you, Ariel, would stand at the North. Together we form a circle – and we are balanced.'

Ariel looked at her three sisters as if they were aliens.

This stuff about elements and balance was all very strange.

She shut her eyes. When she opened them, she thought, everything would be exactly as it had been. They would go downstairs to breakfast and nobody would say anything about magic or powers ever again.

Ariel opened her eyes again and saw that her sisters were all looking intently at her. 'So – what's my power?' she asked.

'You work with the element of Air,' explained Flame. 'You will be able to create great winds and make things float in the sky.'

'Fab-fantastic!'

The Sprite Sisters laughed.

'How long have you all been able to do magic?' asked Ariel.

'Since our ninth birthdays,' replied Ash, who was ten and a half.

'Oh,' said Ariel. 'You never told me.'

'We had to wait until you were nine and you got your own power,' said Ash.

'So that's why I can lift things in the air today. . .' said Ariel.

'Yes, that's right – you were born at two minutes to midnight, which is why you did not have your powers at the party last night,' said Flame.

The four sisters were silent for a moment.

'Listen, pumpkin – there's something else,' said Flame.

'What?'

'It is really, really important that you keep this magical power secret; that you do not tell anyone – even Mum and Dad.'

'But I want to tell Mummy,' said Ariel. 'I always tell her things.'

'I know,' said Flame. 'But you mustn't – really.'

'Why not?'

'Because Mum and Dad do not have magic powers and if they know we have, they will be frightened,' explained Flame. 'The only people who understand about magical powers are people who have them; that's just the way it is.'

'I'd still like to tell Mummy.' Ariel pushed out her bottom lip.

'I know it seems hard,' said Ash. 'Maybe one day you will be able to – perhaps when you are bigger – but not now.'

'Well, who else has magical powers?' asked Ariel.

'Grandma,' said Marina. 'Well, she did when she was young.'

'Grandma?' squeaked Ariel. 'I don't believe you!'

Her sisters laughed.

'It was Grandma who told me what the tingling in my fingers was, on my ninth birthday,' said Flame. 'She'd just come back to live with us here after Grandad had died and she put me to bed that evening. She was sitting here on my bed, like we are now. She asked me if my fingers were tingly and I told her they'd been feeling funny all day. I'd wiggled them about, but the tingling just got stronger.

'Then Grandma told me that I had a magic power, just like she did. I did not know what she meant – I thought she was joking. I said to her, "Don't be silly, Grandma – that's the sort of thing you read about in stories! People don't really have magic powers!"

'But she was serious,' continued Flame. 'She told me that if I pointed my finger and directed the tingly feeling, I would be able to use my magic.

'She told me that it was very important to keep this power a secret. When I asked her why, she said, "If people find out that you have magic power, your power will fade. If you want to keep the power, you must hide it."

'Ariel, she is the only person in the whole world, apart from us three, who you can talk to about your power.'

Ariel had been staring at Flame, and by now her eyes were so wide they looked as if they'd pop out.

'Phew! Thank goodness I can tell someone.' Ariel thought for a moment. 'But if Grandma once had magical powers, why don't Mummy and Daddy?'

'We don't know – it's just one of those things.' Marina shrugged her shoulders. 'Grandma told us that magic powers run through the Sprite family: some of the Sprites have them and some don't. I don't think Dad has them, and Mum's not a Sprite, is she?'

'Did Sidney Sprite have magic powers?' asked Ariel. Sidney Sprite was their great-great-grandfather.

'Grandma says he did,' nodded Ash, tucking her hair behind her ear.

'Marina, did you get a tingling in your fingers, too, when you were nine?' asked Ariel.

'Yes,' replied Marina. 'Flame told me what it was. At first, I thought everybody had magic powers, then I learned from Grandma that we were special.'

'What about you, Ash?'

'Same thing,' replied Ash. 'I was lucky as I was able to talk to Grandma, Marina and Flame. I think it must have been hard for Flame, though, being the first.'

The three younger sisters looked at Flame. She was silent for a moment, then nodded.

'Yes, it was,' she agreed. 'I often felt different from other people. Now I know that my sisters are the same as me, which feels good.'

'We're *all* a bit odd!' said Marina and her sisters laughed.

'I think our powers may grow much stronger, now that Ariel has hers,' said Flame. 'I think things could start to happen to us.'

'Like what?' asked Marina.

'I don't know,' said Flame. 'I just get the feeling that things will change now that we all have our powers.'

'You sometimes see things that are going to happen in the future, don't you?' said Marina.

'Hmm,' nodded Flame.

'Wow!' said Ariel. 'This sounds like it's going to be fun!'

'Listen, Ariel,' said Flame. 'There's one more thing to remember. It's very important.'

Ariel looked at the faces of her three older sisters. They all looked so serious, she thought.

'Our magic must only ever be used for good – never to hurt anyone or cause harm,' continued Flame. 'And you must not play with your power; it could be dangerous.'

Ariel looked down at her hands with a frown. 'Okay,' she said.

'You'll soon get used to it,' said Flame, giving her little sister a hug.

The Sprite Sisters sat cross-legged on Flame's bed facing each other.

'We're in a circle,' said Flame, sitting as straight as a dancer. She looked down and thought for a few seconds. 'I think we should hold hands.'

'Okay,' the others agreed. One by one, the four sisters took each others' hands. As Flame took Marina's hand, the circle was complete.

Flame shut her eyes.

'We call in our power,' she said. 'We call it in – NOW!'

For a moment, nothing happened. Marina, Ash and Ariel looked at one another and grinned. Flame kept her eyes shut.

'It feels all tingly,' giggled Ariel.

Then, suddenly, without any warning – *whooooshh!* A huge bolt of bright blue light surged through their arms and bodies. It pulsed round and round the circle they had made.

'Crikey!' said Marina.

'Cool!' said Ash.

'It's beautiful!' said Ariel.

'It's the Circle of Power,' smiled Flame, opening her eyes. 'Grandma told me this might happen. She said if we all came together in a circle, our power would grow stronger. Whatever happens, we must hold together as sisters – hold the Circle of Power.'

The four sisters looked at one another and down at the bright blue light surging through their arms and hands. For half a minute, they felt the power in the light as they held the circle. Then they let go – and the light subsided.

For a while the Sprite Sisters sat silent on the bed. Flame and Marina shook their hands, as if to loosen them up. Ash stared at her hands, back and front. Ariel poked one of her fingers.

Then Flame turned and looked deep into her little sister's eyes. Ariel blinked at Flame.

'You're going to say something important to me,' said Ariel. 'You always look serious when you say something important.'

Marina and Ash smiled.

Flame nodded. 'Ariel, do you promise that you will keep this secret and that you will never misuse your power?'

'I promise,' she said, in her breathy voice.

CHAPTER TWO

ARIEL'S FIRST MAGIC

SINCE ANYONE could remember, Sprites had lived at Sprite Towers. The Sprite Sisters were born in the house, just like their father and his father and his father before him.

It was the sisters' great-great-grandfather, Sidney Sprite, the famous toffee manufacturer, who had built the magnificent house in 1910. Since then, four generations of Sprite children had slid down the banisters that surrounded the wide mahogany staircase at the heart of the house. Countless games of tag had been played across the rolling lawns and through the trees. Wonderful games of hide-and-seek had been enjoyed from the attics right down to the cellars. There was always somewhere new to explore.

Sprite Towers was a landmark, its high, circular towers visible for miles around – and it was a happy house. True, it was not as grand now as it had been in Sidney's time – some of the furniture looked a little battered and there were rooms that could do with a good lick of paint – but everyone who came there thought of it as happy. The seven members of the Sprite family who lived there now loved their home.

Sprite Towers was its own world. And, each night, as everyone settled to sleep in their beds, you could almost hear the old house giving up a contented sigh.

On this particular Sunday morning, the day after the girls' birthday party and the morning that Ariel discovered her magic power, the birds were singing and the sky was blue. Everyone at Sprite Towers was going cheerfully about their business.

Flame was sitting on the stone step outside the kitchen door reading the newspaper. She cared about things and wanted to know what was happening in the world. The sun shone on her copper-coloured hair as she looked up and gazed around. She loved the peace and quiet of the garden.

Ash was trundling a wheelbarrow over the lawn, wearing her old straw garden hat. She liked to grow things and was happiest in the garden.

Their father, Colin Sprite, great-grandson of Sidney Sprite, and a tall, kindly man, walked behind her carrying a tray of courgette seedlings. Ash looked remarkably like her father: he, too, had chestnut-brown hair and soft brown eyes.

Behind them, Bert the sausage dog lolloped along. A moment later, Dad and Ash disappeared behind the big beech hedge that surrounded the vegetable garden.

Meanwhile, in the big, stone-floored kitchen, Marilyn, the girls' grandmother, was preparing vegetables for Sunday lunch at the sink. You could tell she had once been a ballet dancer by the way she stood so straight and tall. In her youth, she had been a famous beauty. Now, her once long, copper-coloured hair had faded to pale strawberry-blond and was cut into a smart bob, but her eyes still flashed green and her slim body had lost none of its grace.

At the kitchen dresser, Marina was sorting out the cutlery that they had used for the barbecue the night before. The noisiest and liveliest of the Sprite Sisters, she was singing and dancing as she did this. She loved to fling her arms about and move her feet: in her mind, she was always singing to thousands of people, up on stage.

Ariel was sitting in the Windsor chair beside the Aga, stroking Pudding, the tabby cat, who lay on her lap. She was watching her mother knead bread dough on the kitchen table. Of all the Sprite Sisters, Ariel looked most like their mother, with her soft face and floaty blond hair. When she grew up, she would have the same petite, curvy figure.

16

Ottalie Sprite smiled at her little daughter. She was half French and loved to cook. Every Sunday morning, the smell of her baking bread wafted through the house and down the garden. The Sprite family loved it.

The Sunday morning peace was not to last long, however.

Suddenly Dad was running across the lawn towards the house, with Ash close behind him. Flame jumped up as he rushed past her and into the kitchen.

'What's the matter?' asked Flame.

'Slugs!' he shouted, waving his arms like windmills.

'Slugs?' said Mum, rubbing the back of her hand against her face and covering it with flour.

'Yes, slugs everywhere!' said Dad. 'We've been invaded! The biggest slugs you ever saw in your life! Great big orange and black slugs are crawling all over the vegetable garden and they're eating everything! Come and see!'

Dad turned and sped off back to the vegetable garden. The girls ran after him. Mum and Grandma stopped their cooking and followed.

The Sprite family peered down at the neat rows of succulent vegetables. There were curly lettuces, tall, pointy lettuces, crispy lettuces, crinkly, red-leaved lettuces – Dad and Ash grew them all. And not just lettuces – cabbages, tomatoes, carrots, potatoes and more. The vegetable garden at Sprite Towers was spectacular.

But now, sure enough, there were huge orange and

black slugs everywhere.

'I've never seen slugs like this in my life,' said Dad, pointing to a monster chomping its way through a tall, pointy lettuce. 'Where on earth have they come from?'

'Urrrgh,' said Flame, standing back.

'Yurrrk!' Marina shuddered.

Mum and Grandma peered down at them, but were reluctant to get too close.

Ash kneeled down amongst the plants and stroked a slimy monster. She wasn't afraid of slugs.

'How did they get here, Dad?' she asked. 'They weren't here yesterday.'

'It's a mystery.' Dad shook his head. 'But if we don't get rid of them, we soon won't have any vegetables left. Look how quickly they're eating the lettuces!'

He pointed to one that had been gnashed to a small stub in a matter of minutes.

This was a serious business: the Sprites were a big family and relied on their home-grown vegetables to feed themselves. The Sprites had a comfortable life, but they were not a rich family. Colin was an architect and Ottalie a music teacher, but their four daughters' school fees and the maintenance of Sprite Towers put a huge strain on their finances. The vegetables were needed.

Even so, Mum and Grandma beat a retreat back to the kitchen. Lunch needed attention and neither had any inclination to start dealing with monster slugs.

Dad bent down beside the slugs and stared.

'Malacology,' announced Flame, above him.

'What's that?' asked Dad, turning to look up at her.

'The study of molluscs – invertebrate creatures with soft, unsegmented bodies, many of which house themselves in shells,' said Flame.

'Er, right,' said Dad. 'Thanks, Flame.'

'That's okay,' she said. 'And people who study molluscs are called malacologists.'

'How do you know stuff like that?' asked Dad.

'Just do,' said Flame. 'I s'pose it's because I like odd facts and I can remember unusual words.'

Ariel crouched down and stared at a humungous slimy slug.

Dad stood up and scratched his head. 'I think I'd better go and look these slugs up on the Internet – I don't know how we're going to deal with this lot.'

And off he hurried, back to the house.

The Sprite Sisters were alone in the vegetable garden, hidden from the house by the large beech hedge. Bert, the sausage dog, pottered about sniffing at things.

'We've got to use our magic powers – fast,' said Ash, standing up.

Ariel squiggled up her face and lifted her hands.

'What are you going to do?' asked Ash.

'I am going to see if I can make the slugs lift up like my teddy bears,' said Ariel.

'Be careful!' said Ash. 'Don't hurt them!'

'Oh no, Ariel – please wait!' said Flame, moving forwards – but it was too late.

Ariel had shut her eyes, opened them and lifted her hands to waist height. As she pointed her two index fingers and lifted her hands a little more, over one hundred slugs rose up from the lettuces and cabbages and hovered in the air. The entire vegetable garden was covered by what looked like a shimmering sheet of orange and black slugs.

'Look at this – two hands!' squeaked Ariel. 'Flying slugs!'

'Oh heck!' said Ash. 'Stay there! Keep your hands still!'

She ran to the garden shed and grabbed two plastic buckets.

'Come on!' she said, handing one to Flame.

'What do want us to do?' asked Marina.

'Collect the slugs of course!' said Ash.

Marina and Flame looked at each other in horror.

'You do it!' said Flame, handing Marina the bucket.

'No, you do it – you're the eldest!' said Marina, handing it back to Flame.

'Oh for heaven's sake, stop bickering and give me some help!' shouted Ash, as she moved up a row of lettuces. Holding her bucket on its side at waist height, she scooped up the hovering slugs.

Flame moved to the edge of the hovering slug sheet and gingerly scooped up one slug. She cringed as it plopped into the bucket.

Ariel giggled and her left hand wobbled. Some of the slugs lost height. Others got higher. She made a swooshy movement with her hands – and the slugs looked like an orange wave floating over the garden.

'Keep still, Ariel!' shouted Ash, as she lunged forward to catch a falling slug and nearly lost her balance.

Marina stood by and watched, her face screwed up in disgust. Flame picked her way slowly along the edge of the vegetable patch, scooping in the odd slug here and there, while Ash hurtled up and the down the rows of lettuces, rapidly filling her bucket with the squelchy creatures.

Bert was going bonkers: he barked and barked and ran round and round in sausage-dog circles. Ash's bucket was soon full of slugs. She carried it to where Ariel was standing and dropped it heavily on the ground.

'Phew!' said Ash. 'Keep going, Ariel!'

Ash grabbed the second bucket from Flame.

'Here, let me take it,' she said, panting and looking into the bucket. 'There's only six slugs in here! I don't understand why you and Marina are so useless.'

The slugs in the bucket on the ground were starting to slither up the inside. Bert stuck in his long doggy nose to sniff them – and jumped back. They smelled revolting, even to a sausage dog.

'Don't let those escape!' shouted Ash, as she dashed off again.

There were still dozens of monster slugs hovering in

mid-air, but Ash was catching them at a record pace now. Soon there was only one left.

Ariel giggled and moved her fingers up and down and watched as she made the last slug move higher and lower.

'Good grief, stop moving your hands about, Ariel!' shouted Ash.

Ariel still laughed, but kept her hands still as Ash scooped up the last slug.

'Now what?' asked Marina.

'What do you mean, now what? You didn't pick up any!' said Flame.

'Well, you only got six!' Marina retorted.

Ash looked around at the vegetable garden. 'Well, the lettuces are safe – the slugs are all out of the vegetable patch,' she said. 'But what on earth do we do with them?'

Ash dropped the second bucket on the ground beside the first one. The slugs were still slithering up the sides of the buckets. She poked them back in with her finger.

'They're escaping!' she said. 'I can't keep them in!'

'Yuuurkk,' said Flame. 'You touched them!'

'Eeehhh,' squirmed Marina, moving back a few paces.

'Oh, come on, stop being such wusses!' hissed Ash. 'We must do something with them before Dad gets back.'

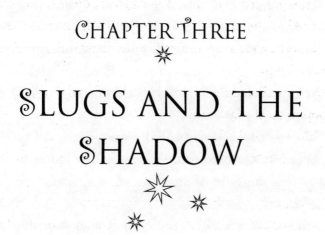

CHAPTER THREE

SLUGS AND THE SHADOW

'WHAT'S ON the other side of the wall just here?' asked Marina, looking up at the high red brick wall that surrounded the entire garden of Sprite Towers. This particular bit bounded the east and south sides of the vegetable garden.

'It's waste ground, covered in nettles,' replied Flame, staring up at the wall. 'There's plenty for slugs to eat – they should be happy over there.'

'How about Ariel flies the slugs over the wall?' suggested Marina.

'Oh yes, goodie!' said Ariel – and immediately lifted her finger.

'Hang on a mo,' said Ash, grabbing Ariel's finger and pushing it down. 'Will the slugs get hurt when they land?'

'They'll have a soft landing on plants,' said Flame.

Marina looked along at the wall. 'There's the little door in the wall in the far corner of the Wild Wood, isn't there? We could get out that way to check they're okay.'

'Yes, but it might be locked,' said Flame. 'I don't think anyone's used it in years.'

'We don't have time to look now – Dad will be back any minute,' said Marina, hands on hips. 'Come on – let's just get the slugs out of the vegetable garden. Go on Ariel – use your powers!'

Ariel focused her eyes on the first bucket of slugs and pointed her finger at it. A bolt of blue light shot out as – *whoosh!* – dozens of slugs flew up into the air and over the top of the wall in a great heave of slime.

'Urgh!' exclaimed Flame and Marina, jumping back.

'Magic powers are so cool!' said Ariel, looking at her stubby pink finger.

'Quick, do this one too!' said Ash, lifting the second bucket towards her.

By the opening in the beech hedge, Bert was waiting expectantly for Dad. His ears pricked and he gave a short bark.

'Dad's coming back – quick!' said Ash.

The second swarm of slugs whooshed over the wall just as Dad raced through the opening.

'Right! Well, I think I've got the answer, girls!' he said as he strode towards them, saw their faces and stopped. 'What are you up to?' he asked, noticing the empty buckets. 'Are you going to collect up the slugs?'

Flame, Marina, Ash and Ariel froze.

'Well?' he asked.

'Er . . . we have, Dad,' said Ash.

Dad spun round and peered at the vegetable patch. There was not a single slug to be seen.

'Where are they?' he asked. 'There were a hundred slugs here ten minutes ago!'

The Sprite Sisters stared at their father.

He stared at them. 'Well?'

'We collected them up,' said Ash.

'We all ran around like mad,' said Marina.

'And we put them in the buckets,' added Ariel.

'You picked up a hundred big slugs?' asked Dad. 'You picked up all those slugs, covered in all that slime. Slithery slugs, hiding under the lettuce leaves?'

Marina and Flame shuddered at the thought.

'Well, *I* did, mostly,' replied Ash. 'I don't mind slugs.'

'And then?'

'And then we put them in the buckets,' said Flame. 'Didn't we?' She nodded at her sisters.

They all nodded back.

'And *then* what did you do?' asked Dad.

Flame, Marina and Ariel looked at Ash. Ash knew

about stuff in the garden, she would know what to say, they thought. She was good at thinking her way out of tight spots too.

Ash blinked at her father. She was still hot from running around. Her face was bright red and her hair stood up like a bird's nest.

'Well, they were in the buckets all together . . .' she said.

'And?'

'And . . . they wiggled about . . .'

'Yes?' Dad raised an eyebrow and crossed his arms.

Flame, Marina and Ariel held their breath. What was Ash going to tell him?

Dad waited. 'Then what?' he asked.

'We threw them over the wall,' said Ash, waving her arm in a big arc.

'Don't be ridiculous!' guffawed Dad. 'I was only gone ten minutes! You couldn't possibly have collected up a hundred slugs and thrown them over the wall! I mean, look at it – it's nearly four metres high!'

'Yes, we did,' said Ash.

Dad stared at Ash.

Ash stared at Dad.

'We did, Dad,' Flame, Marina and Ariel chorused in agreement.

'Um,' said Dad, rubbing his chin and peering down at the empty buckets. 'This is all very strange. I was only gone ten minutes . . .' Dad scratched his head. 'It's all very odd . . . Oh well – just as long as they don't get back into the vegetable garden.'

At that moment, Grandma rang the brass ship's bell that hung outside the kitchen door.

'Lunchtime!' shouted Marina.

The Sprite Sisters didn't need telling twice. They dashed through the opening in the beech hedge, over the lawn, up on to the terrace and burst in through the kitchen door in a great heap.

'Wash your hands, then come and sit down, girls,' said Grandma, looking at them suspiciously. She had a feeling they'd been up to some magic.

The older girls knew she would ask them about this later, but right now it was Sunday lunch. They were safe for a while.

'Whatever have you been doing?' asked Mum, as the girls sat down at the table, giggling.

'We put the slugs over the wall,' said Ariel.

'How?' said Mum, placing the gravy jug on the table.

Ariel was just about to tell Mum about whooshing the slugs with her magic powers, when Ash gave her a sharp nudge. 'Sssh,' she whispered.

Ariel gave her a cross look. 'All right, all right,' she said.

Luckily, Mum was thinking about lunch, not slugs.

Dad came into the kitchen, washed his hands and sat down at the head of the long oak table. In front of him was a huge joint of roast beef on a big white plate. He picked up the carving knife and fork and began to carve the joint into neat slices. The table was covered with food – puffy Yorkshire puddings, dishes of crispy roast potatoes and home-grown vegetables and the jug of deep brown gravy. It smelled wonderful.

As the Sprite family ate lunch, Dad tried several times to ask his daughters again how they had collected up the slugs and got them over the wall, but each time he mentioned the subject everyone said they felt sick.

'No, Dad – *please!* Not while we're eating!' they chorused.

His wife smiled at him; his mother smiled at him; his four daughters smiled at him – and he gave up. He was a man outnumbered by women.

'Well, I don't know – I was only gone ten minutes,' he said yet again, shaking his head. 'It's a mystery. And how did they get there anyway – that's what I'd like to know?'

The Sprite family was silent.

Dad looked at Bert, sitting in his long sausage-dog basket; Bert looked at Dad, raised his long ears, then lay down and went to sleep.

After lunch, Grandma, Mum and Dad sat on the terrace, drank coffee and read the Sunday newspapers.

Flame and Ash were swinging on two tractor tyres that hung from thick ropes attached to the lime tree at the east side of the lawn. They were waiting for Mum, Dad and Grandma to go back inside before they set off to see if they could get through the door in the wall. They wanted to make sure the slugs were safe and sound.

Marina and Ariel played with their rabbits and guinea pigs on the grass and did cat's cradle with a piece of string.

The birds were singing, the sky was blue and everybody at Sprite Towers was enjoying the tranquility of a warm afternoon in the sunshine.

There was a moment, however – a very fleeting moment, so quick you would barely notice it – when a dark shadow seemed to pass over the house and garden. For a split second, everything went dark.

Everyone looked up and shivered – but saw nothing. There was not a cloud in the sky. There were no planes overhead, no huge flocks of birds – nothing that would create a shadow over Sprite Towers.

But it felt dark all of a sudden – and for one brief moment, the Sprite family had a sense of unease, even in the peace of their garden.

As the shadow passed over, Grandma felt stony cold.

'It's suddenly gone chilly,' she shivered, hugging herself and rubbing the sides of her arms. She looked up and thought how strange it was that she should feel cold on such a glorious afternoon.

Under the lime tree, Flame asked Ash, 'Did you see that?'

'What – that shadow?' said Ash. 'I felt it, rather than saw it.'

Flame looked up at the sky. 'It was weird.'

'I feel cold,' said Ash. 'Come on, let's get the others and make sure the slugs are okay.'

At Sprite Towers, it was not the weather that had changed. Something far more sinister was happening.

Unknown to the family, at the precise moment that Sprite Towers was cast in darkness, a tall, elegant woman in her late sixties was getting out of a car and walking towards another big house one mile away. Her long, pale blond hair was swept back in a chignon on the nape of her neck and her hands were perfectly manicured.

The woman stood on the wide gravel drive and gazed around her, as if looking at the house for the first time. She looked up at the sky. Behind her, people scurried about carrying dozens of cases and hat boxes into the house.

As the front door opened, the woman smiled a grim smile. She was not thinking of the welcome that awaited her here, however: she was thinking of the Sprite family. She was smiling at the prospect of spoiling their happy life at Sprite Towers.

When Flame had told her sister Ariel that morning that no one in the world, apart from their grandmother, knew they had magical powers, she was wrong. There was someone else who suspected their secret – and she was out for revenge.

CHAPTER FOUR

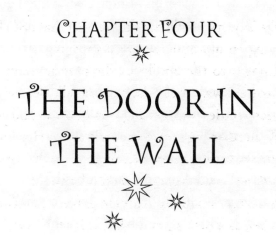

THE DOOR IN THE WALL

'COME ON!' said Flame. 'Let's see if we can get through the door in the wall and check on the slugs.'

'But we don't have a key,' said Marina.

'We don't know for *certain* that it's locked,' Flame replied.

The four Sprite Sisters got on their bicycles, which were propped against the wall outside the kitchen, and cycled over the wide lawn, past the secret garden and the summer house, past the field with the sheep grazing and down towards the trees. They were heading for the Wild Wood, at the south-west corner of Sprite Towers' grounds. It was too dense to cycle through, so the Sprite Sisters left their bikes at the edge and walked.

The Wild Wood was full of pine trees, which grew tall and dark. The air smelled damp and fusty – no grass or plants here, only pine needles densely covering the ground. There were dozens of rabbit warrens and several foxes' earths. Mindful of the branches poking out and the holes underfoot, the sisters carefully picked their way through the trees until they saw the high red-brick wall that bounded Sprite Towers.

'There it is!' said Ash, pointing through the trees.

And there was the door in the wall: a small, arched wooden door, with flaking blue-grey paint, rusty hinges and bolts and over two metres of wall above it. The trees had thinned out here and in front of the door were huge clumps of brambles.

'We can't get through – we'll get scratched to death,' said Ash. 'Why don't we go out of the grounds and cycle around the outside of the wall instead?'

'That's boring!' said Marina. 'We can get through: I'll make a path by shrivelling up the plants. Stand aside, please.'

She held out her right hand and moved it across the brambles from left to right, back and forth. The huge plants started to wilt as Marina sucked out every bit of moisture, using her magic power. Within a minute the way was clear: the brambles lay limp on the ground.

The sisters picked their way through the shrivelled plants to the door.

'I don't remember this ever being open,' said Flame, looking the old wooden door up and down. There were two large rusty bolts drawn across at the top and bottom and in the middle was a huge old lock, but no key. 'Let's try the bolts first, in case it's not locked.' She reached up to the bolt at the top of the arched door, but it was rusted in and would not shift.

'Let me try,' said Marina. 'Just stand back a bit.' She placed her hand over the bolt and closed her eyes.

Her sisters stepped back. As if from nowhere, a sticky, oily liquid came out of Marina's hands. A few seconds later, she drew back the bolt: it moved freely and easily.

'Right, bottom one now,' she said, bending down. The second bolt released. 'That's it!' she cried, giving the door a push. It didn't move. Flame and Ash came forward and pushed with all their strength, but the door stayed firmly shut.

'Okay, it's locked – we have to find the key,' said Flame, rubbing her shoulder.

Ash stared at the door for a few seconds. 'Hang on – I think I know where it may be!' she said. 'I've just remembered. Dad has a drawer for keys in the stables. Why didn't I think of that before? I'll go and see if it's there.'

And she strode off through the trees to get her bicycle.

Minutes later she returned, holding a huge, rusty key. 'We may be in luck,' she said. 'Let's see if it's the right one.' She placed the key in the lock and tried to turn it anti-clockwise. The key slotted in, but would not turn.

'The lock's completely rusted up,' said Flame. 'This may need a bit of oil, too.'

Marina moved forward and held her hand over the lock. 'There you go,' she said after a moment, and wiped her hands clean on the grass.

When Ash turned the key this time, it moved with ease. The lock opened with a satisfying clunk.

Flame pulled on the round metal handle. The door creaked open. Kicking down the grass in front of the door, Flame managed to open it just enough for the Sprite Sisters to squeeze through.

And there they were, suddenly – outside the wall and outside the world of Sprite Towers. In front of them were more big clumps of nettles and brambles; beyond that a grassy track and then fields. Hardly anyone ever used the footpath running around this side of Sprite Towers. Occasionally the Sprite Sisters came down here, but there was enough to keep them busy in the house and grounds of Sprite Towers.

The Sprite Sisters picked their way through the undergrowth and on to the grassy track. They walked eastwards, with the wall on their left side, back towards where the vegetable garden lay behind the wall.

'Look!' squeaked Ariel, jumping up and down. 'The slugs!'

There they were, in all their slimy glory, chomping away at the nettles and slithering off over the grass. For the second time that day, there were slugs everywhere.

'Some are moving towards the wall!' shouted Marina.

'Oh heck,' said Ash. 'They're after the lettuces again. We'd better move them back here. Quick, Ariel!'

'Bring them together on the track here and I'll burn a circle round them on the grass,' said Flame.

Ariel was delighted to be using her new-found magic powers again that day. In a flash, the orange and black monster slugs rose from the ground, hurtled together and landed, *kerflup*, on the track in a huge heap.

'Okay, let's make sure they stay here for now,' said Flame. 'Stand back everyone.'

She started to walk clockwise around the slugs in a wide circle. As she did so, she pointed her right hand down at the grass. A bolt of bright white flame, pencil-thin, like a laser, shot out of her finger and scorched the grass. The grass sizzled and smoked. Flame walked round the pile of slugs several times, until she had made a wide circle of burnt grass around them.

'Why are you doing that?' asked Ariel.

'It's a circle of fire,' explained Flame. 'Slugs don't like burnt grass and won't cross over it unless they have to – so they'll stay within the circle, for the moment at least. It'll give us time to think what we are going to do with them. Mum will want us in for music practice now.'

Ash looked thoughtful. 'The slugs will be safe here,' she said. 'I'll just get them some nettles to eat.'

Using her earth power, Ash uprooted a dozen big nettle plants and Ariel tossed them into the slug circle.

'We can come back and check them tomorrow,' she said, watching as the slugs began to tuck into the nettles. 'They'll be safe until then. Come on, we'd better go in now – Mum will be looking for us.'

The Sprite Sisters took a last look at the circle of fire and the heap of slugs, then hurried back through the door in the wall and pulled it shut. Ash locked it and went off to take the key back to the stables, grabbing her bike at the edge of the Wild Wood.

'Hang on a mo,' said Marina to Flame and Ariel, as they looked at the ground in front of the door. 'I'd better put these brambles back or Dad may notice we've been here.'

She lifted her hands towards the wilted plants and closed her eyes. In an instant, the plants filled with water again and stood up tall and strong. The whole place looked as it did when the Sprite Sisters had found it.

'No one would ever know we've been here!' laughed Flame, amazed at the healthy-looking brambles. 'Well done, Marina.'

'It's very useful to have magic powers, I think,' said Ariel. Flame and Marina laughed and the three of them began to pick their way back through the Wild Wood. At the edge, they jumped on their bicycles and sped back home to the house. Ash caught up with them as they raced across the wide, rolling lawn.

The late afternoon sun shone in the sky. As the Sprite family settled down to tea on the terrace, the grassy track at the side of Sprite Towers had another visitor. A small, bearded man was cycling slowly along the track. On his left was a high red-brick wall. On his back was a large rucksack full of special jars. On the front of the bicycle was a wire-framed basket fixed over the front wheel, and in this were a variety of canisters.

Dr Phil Lemon, zoologist and malacologist, was on a slug hunt. On Sunday afternoons, he often cycled out to the country from the university where he worked to look for rare species of slugs. Phil was an expert on slugs. He had been researching them for years. He loved the slimy creatures and was always optimistic that one day he would have a big find.

So there he was, late on this sunny June afternoon, pottering along the grassy track that ran down one side of the house that was marked on the map as *Sprite Towers*. It was the first time Phil had been there. He hummed happily as he followed the curve of the wall and noticed, ahead, a small arched door.

Then, suddenly, he jammed on the brakes.

What is *that*? he thought to himself.

In front of him, on the grassy track, was a large circle of burnt grass and . . . and inside that was a pile of monster orange and black slugs, chomping stinging nettles.

Phil narrowed his eyes. He got off his bicycle, put it down and walked towards the circle. His eyes glazed over and his mouth dropped open. He made a strange sound – a sort of amazed 'Urgh?'

Then he said, 'Oh my goodness! Oh great heavens! Oh my sainted aunts!' And he leaned over the smouldering circle of ash on the ground and picked up a huge slug.

He held the slug close to his face.

'Where on earth have you come from?' he said. 'Are you what I think you are?'

The slug peered back, slimy and silent.

Phil leaped into action. There was not a moment to lose. Within a few minutes he had photographed the slugs on the ground, collected them all up and stored them safely in his ventilated jars and canisters. If he left them in the charred circle on the ground, they would soon eat all the nettles and be hungry – then they'd find their way over the burnt grass to look for food. He might never find them again.

He looked around. There was no one about. There were only trees, fields, a huge red brick wall and a small door.

Phil knew these slugs were not native to those parts.

But who had burned this ground? And how on earth had these slugs got here?

Phil did not stop to think about this now. He had more important things on his mind. As he pedalled furiously back to the university, he was thinking about making the slugs safe – and about what he would say to the newspapers.

This was a find indeed! It would make his career. It would make him famous – he, Dr Phil Lemon!

Meanwhile, the Sprite Sisters sat on the terrace and ate sandwiches and large pieces of cake and drank glasses of homemade lemonade.

Then it was time for music practice. In a few days' time, they would perform together at the school concert. Their school – Drysdale's School – was taking part in the National Schools Music Competition. Eight schools were competing in the regional heats, with a chance to go through to the national final. The judges had already attended concerts at the seven other schools, and on Friday it would be Drysdale's turn at last. After the concert, the judges would choose the top school from the region. The winning school's musicians would then go forward to the final in London at the end of the summer term.

Hopes and dreams were riding high at Drysdale's, which had some fine young musicians and singers.

Amongst them were the Sprite Sisters. Apart from hoping to win the competition, they were really looking forward to the chance of spending a weekend in London.

Music was a big part of life at Sprite Towers. Ottalie Sprite was a gifted pianist and singer and a well-known teacher. She gave piano lessons at the house and taught the senior pupils at Drysdale's. She was also one of the people responsible for organising the inter-schools competition. Her daughters had inherited her musical talent and each played several instruments.

That Sunday evening, the Sprite Sisters were excited – and slugs were soon forgotten. It was now only five days until the concert. It would be the first time they performed together in public – and they would be amongst the stars of the show.

They settled down to practise in the drawing-room. Five music stands and chairs were set up: one for each of the girls and one for Mum, who conducted them.

That evening, Dad and Grandma sat on the big cream sofas and listened. Bert listened too, sitting on Grandma's lap. The family loved this room, with its pale duck-egg blue walls hung with paintings, the elegant stone fireplace and the huge bookcase stuffed full of books.

The Sprite Sisters played beautifully. Nobody lost her temper or got upset. Ariel held her silver flute up above her right shoulder, put her top lip over her bottom lip and blew into the mouthpiece with the look of someone who would float away with its soft, airy sound.

'Ariel, focus!' said Mum, smiling.

Ariel frowned with concentration.

'Well done,' said Mum, as her little daughter sailed through a tricky passage.

Joining the flute on the top notes, Flame played her violin with intense concentration and spark. Bringing in the middle notes, Marina enjoyed the mellow tones of the viola and played with feeling and movement. Supplying the bass sounds, Ash was blissfully happy playing her cello. She loved its deep, woody tone and the feeling of drawing the horsehair bow across the tight metal strings.

The Sprite Sisters brought their music to a wonderful climax – and the concert was over.

'Bravo!' said Dad.

'Lovely!' Grandma clapped.

'Take a bow!' said Mum with a smile.

The Sprite Sisters stood up to face their audience, bowed and smiled.

'Right, put your instruments away, get your bags ready for the morning and then straight off to bed,' said Mum.

'Grandma, will you tuck us up tonight?' asked Ariel.

'Of course,' smiled Grandma. 'Is that all right with you, Ottalie?'

'Certainly! Thank you,' said Mum.

Mum and Grandma look so different, thought Flame, as she put her violin back in its case. Mum was small and pretty and soft. She didn't *look* fierce, but Flame and her sisters knew better. Ottalie Sprite was strict, despite being playful and loving.

Grandma, on the other hand, *looked* as if she could be fierce – and sometimes she was, thought Flame. She was not sure she had ever seen her grandmother look untidy, even wearing a dressing gown: Marilyn Sprite was an elegant woman, with her chic strawberry-blond bob. Flame knew that her grandmother's hair had once been the same deep copper colour as her own, and that, of the four granddaughters, she was the most like Grandma, in shape and sharpness of wit, as well as colouring.

Flame looked at Ash, as she took the music sheets off the stands. Ash resembled Dad. They both look like trees, Flame mused – Ash was named after one. They were tall, broad-shouldered and strong and not easily knocked over. Flame liked Ash's calmness and her quiet ability to just get on with things when the other girls were making a fuss.

Flame glanced at Marina. Grandma always said she looked like the girls' grandfather, Sheldon. Flame had only known him as an older man, with silvery-white hair. But she had seen photographs of him when he was young: Marina had his bright blue eyes and curly black hair.

'Ah, he was such a handsome man, your grandfather!'

Grandma would say, wistfully, when she looked at old photographs of them together.

For many years, she and Grandad had lived in the south of France. When he died several years ago, a corrupt lawyer stole most of their money, so Grandma came back to live with her son and his family at Sprite Towers.

It was around that time, Flame remembered, that she had first felt the magic power in her hands. She was just nine years old. Grandma had come to her and told her what it was. Since then, they had often talked about it. Now Ariel was nine – and Flame sensed Grandma would talk to them all this evening.

Soon everything was ready for school in the morning and it was time for the girls to say goodnight to their parents.

'Right, bathtime!' said Grandma.

The Sprite Sisters and Grandma went through the hallway past the portrait of Sidney Sprite, the founder of Sprite Towers, which hung on the wall at the bottom of the wide mahogany staircase.

Sidney's portrait, which was enclosed in a huge, ornate gilt frame, showed him as a whiskery, jolly sort of chap, a man who enjoyed eating toffees and telling good stories. He was also, the girls had always been told, a keen astronomer and liked to watch the night sky from his towers.

It was family tradition that everybody said goodnight

to Sidney as they went upstairs for the night. Nobody knew when the tradition had started, but Dad could remember doing it when he was a young boy, and Grandma remembered Grandad saying he'd done it too, as a lad.

'Night, Sidney!' the Sprite Sisters said, as they swung round the acorn-shaped newel post at the bottom of the staircase. Then they grabbed the banister rail and piled up the wide mahogany stairs.

The sisters raced up to the second floor of the house and then argued about who was first in the bathroom. That evening it was Ash who won. Grandma followed at a sensible pace.

Sprite Towers was such a big house that each of the sisters had their own bedroom on the second floor. Mum and Dad had a bedroom on the first floor. Grandma had two rooms there: a bedroom and a sitting room with her own television, for when she wanted some peace and quiet on her own.

That evening, on the second floor, Flame, Marina and Ash went off to have showers in the bathroom at one end of the corridor, while Grandma ran a bath for Ariel at the other.

'Will you tell us one of your stories tonight, Grandma?' asked Ariel.

'Yes,' smiled Grandma. 'But let's get you in the bath first.'

44

* * *

Soon Ariel was wrapped in a big towel and chatting to Grandma in the bathroom. Ash poked her head round the door. 'I'm done,' she said, her short brown hair tousled and damp.

'Grandma's going to tell us a story!' said Ariel. 'Whose bed will you sit on, Grandma?'

'Yours tonight, pickle. Come on – let's dry those feet. Don't forget to clean your teeth, Ash.'

'We never went back to check on the slugs!' Marina said to Flame as they walked along the corridor to Ariel's bedroom.

'Oh heck – I just forgot, with music practice and all that,' said Flame.

'I hope they haven't got back into the vegetable garden,' said Marina.

'Maybe they've all slithered off, or been captured by a crazy slug collector,' mused Flame.

'Yeah, right – and maybe we'll be on the telly tomorrow morning, too!' laughed Marina.

At the very moment that Flame and Marina were making their way along the corridor to Ariel's bedroom, a few miles away the slugs were slithering around a huge glass tank in a university laboratory.

Phil Lemon was talking on the telephone. He was very excited and he waved his arms about as he spoke. 'Yes,

45

I'm absolutely *certain* it's them!' he said. 'I'll see you in the morning then!' He put the phone down. 'We're going to be famous, my beauties!' he said to the slugs, but the slugs weren't listening.

CHAPTER FIVE

GRANDMA HAS A WORD

FIVE MINUTES later, Ariel sat in her pink bed wearing her powder-pink pyjamas. Flame, Marina and Ash sat on top of the bed, along the wall, in their dressing gowns. Grandma sat on the end, facing them.

'Now, what happened today?' she asked, looking at each granddaughter in turn.

'What – with the slugs?' asked Marina.

'Yes,' nodded Grandma.

The sisters laughed; Grandma smiled.

'It was *so* funny!' squeaked Ariel, lifting her dimply hands in the air. 'I made them float in the air, like this.'

'Careful,' said Grandma, taking Ariel's hands and lowering them down to the bed.

'Ash ran round and round the garden collecting the floating slugs in a bucket, and they were climbing out and squirming,' continued Ariel, wiggling her hands. 'Dad was coming back any minute, so I whooshed the slugs over the top of the garden wall! It's ever so high!'

Marina was curling up with laughter. 'Dad only just missed seeing the slugs hurtle through the air – it was so funny! He asked Ash what happened and she didn't know what to say!'

'What did you tell him, Ash?' asked Grandma.

'I said we'd collected the slugs in buckets and thrown them over the wall – but I don't think he believed me,' giggled Ash. 'Then you rang the lunch bell and we all dashed off – and I've managed to avoid him since then.'

'Are you cross with us, Grandma?' asked Ariel. 'We did save the vegetables.'

The sisters were quiet.

'No, I'm not cross,' chuckled Grandma. 'It sounds funny – all that dashing round the garden – but I think you need to reflect.'

A look of seriousness came over Grandma's face. 'You all have these wonderful powers. You must always think very hard before you use them, for two reasons. First, because they must be kept secret: nobody but us must know. You understand that, don't you?'

Grandma looked at Flame, Marina and Ash. She'd had many conversations about magic powers with her elder granddaughters in the last few years.

'Yes.' Flame, Ash and Marina nodded.

'And you, Ariel?' Grandma looked at her youngest granddaughter.

'Why must it be a secret, Grandma?' asked Ariel. 'It's funny to lift things up. I don't know anyone else who can do that.'

'Very, very few people can do that, Ariel,' said Grandma. 'That's why you must keep it a secret. If people find out you have a special power, they will treat you differently. They may be afraid of you – may even shun you. They don't know that you won't cause them harm.

'More importantly, if your power is publicly exposed – you will lose it. You may never find it again. At this moment in your lives you are young and your power is not yet fully formed – especially yours, Ariel. It is not strong enough to withstand public exposure. Your power is vulnerable. It will strengthen as you get older, but you must give it time. Guard your magic carefully: keep it close and keep it hidden, if you want it to grow. Do you understand?'

Ariel looked hard at her grandmother. 'I think so, Grandma,' she replied.

'Your sisters will help you, won't you girls?' said Grandma.

'Yes,' the older girls nodded.

'But why can't Mum and Dad know?' asked Ariel. 'I'd

like to tell Mummy about making things float in the air.'

'I know, sweetheart,' said her grandmother. 'But the same thing applies with your parents: talk about your power or try to impress people with it – even your mother and father – and you will find it weakens. You girls are very lucky: you can talk to and learn from each other and you can share your thoughts and feelings with me.'

'Dad is a Sprite though – wouldn't he understand?' asked Ash.

'The only people who understand what it's like to have magic powers are other people with magic powers,' replied Grandma.

Ash nodded. 'That makes sense,' she said.

'What's the second reason, Grandma?' asked Flame. She always remembered things in conversations.

'The other thing to remember is that you may lose your powers if you do not use them wisely and kindly,' said Grandma. 'I know, because I once had special powers like you – and I lost them.'

Flame, Marina and Ash knew this, but none of them had ever found out why. Grandma had always told them she would tell them the story when Ariel came into her power. They had waited for this moment; Flame had waited for four years.

'You have been very patient, girls – Flame especially,' smiled Grandma.

'Tell us the story, Grandma,' said Marina.

'Yes, tell us what happened, please,' said Ash. They all huddled together on the bed.

'When I was a little girl and I got to my ninth birthday, strange things began to happen to me,' said Grandma. 'Like you, I started to get a tingling in my fingers. I found I could move things – pull things towards me, push them away or make them change shape.

'My grandmother came to me – just as I have done to you – and told me about my magic power. She had this power too. Now, as you know, my grandmother was a Sprite: she was the younger sister of Sidney Sprite. The magic power that I had, and which you have running through your veins, has been passed down through the Sprite family for hundreds and hundreds of years. Nobody knows where it comes from, or why the Sprites have it.

'Now, your great-great-grandfather, Sidney Sprite had it, but he was unusual: normally it is the Sprite women who have had the magic powers, rather than the men,' continued Grandma. 'Sidney had three sisters – Elisa, Margaret and Alice, who was my grandmother. There were two other brothers, Stanley and Russell, but I was always told they did not have the magic power, and neither did Elisa. It seems that Sidney, Margaret and Alice, however, all inherited the magic and each passed it down through their own families.'

'Did Dad inherit it?' asked Flame.

'No, I don't think so,' replied Grandma. 'I think I would have known.'

'What about Grandad Sheldon?' asked Marina.

'No, I don't think he had magic power either.'

'But if everybody keeps it secret, how would you know if they have it or not?' asked Flame.

'That's a good question,' smiled Grandma. 'The answer is, if you have power, you just know if you meet someone else who has it, too. You can feel it in them. They don't need to tell you. As you grow older, you girls will sense it if someone around you has magic powers: you will learn to recognise them.'

The Sprite Sisters thought about this for a second.

'So what happened as you grew up?' asked Ash.

'Well, as I got older, I became very confident,' said Grandma. 'I was an only child and my parents adored me. I had long, copper-coloured hair like Flame. I was a gifted dancer and, of course, I became a ballerina. I had a wonderful time with the ballet. I danced all over the world and had such fun.'

'And you wore lots of feathers,' prompted Marina.

'Yes, lots of feathers,' said Grandma.

'And sparkly outfits?' asked Marina. She loved the idea of the stage and the costumes and always enjoyed hearing Grandma's stories about her life as a ballerina.

'Lots of sparkle,' agreed Grandma.

'Did you have lots of boyfriends?' asked Ariel.

'Lots of admirers, yes.' Grandma smiled. 'I used to get sent flowers all the time.'

'So, what happened with your magic power?' asked Flame.

'Well, one of the other dancers was a spiteful girl, always jealous of the other dancers – and particularly of me.'

'Why was she jealous of you, Grandma?' asked Ash.

'Because I was considered to be the best dancer in the *corps de ballet* and she thought she was,' said Grandma. 'She was a very good dancer. We were rivals.'

'What was her name?' asked Ash.

'Glenda,' said Grandma.

Grandma sat silent for a moment after she had said this name. A feeling of coldness came over her. She shuddered. 'Oh, I've gone all shivery again – second time today,' she smiled, rubbing her hands on her arms. 'Now where was I?'

'You were telling us Glenda was jealous of you,' said Ash.

'Oh, yes,' said Grandma. 'Well, she was jealous of so many people – but I was the one she hated most because I was given the best dancing roles. She couldn't bear that I was chosen over her. She'd get so nasty, though she was as sweet as pie to the choreographer and manager. There were two sides to her. They got the sweet side: I got the nasty side.

'Then, one day I discovered that Glenda and I were

related. I had told my mother and father about her when I'd been home to see them. My mother recognised her name – Glenda Frost, as she was then. Mother told me that Glenda was the granddaughter of Margaret Sprite, my grandmother's sister. So, although we had different surnames, she was a Sprite, too, by blood. She even looked a bit like me, though *her* hair was long and blond.

'When I got back to the theatre, I told Glenda we were second cousins – but it made no difference. She said she already knew, although I never found out how she knew. She was still jealous and cold. She was the coldest person I ever met.'

Grandma was silent for a few seconds, deep in thought.

Then she said, 'Once I realised Glenda was a Sprite, I was much more wary of her.'

'Why?' asked Marina.

'Because I sensed that she might have magic powers, like me,' said Grandma. 'I knew she could hurt me. My grandmother had always told me that there was a branch of the Sprite family who used their power against people, particularly against other Sprites. She told me these Sprites had broken the Sprite Code of Honour that said all Sprites should use their magic wisely and kindly. Over the years, theirs became a dark, cruel power and it grew very strong.'

'So there are good Sprites and bad Sprites?' said Ash, her brown eyes wide.

'Yes – and it's important to know the difference,' said

Grandma. 'The bad Sprites play by different rules. Unlike you, they can use their magic unkindly without losing their powers – which means they can be very dangerous.'

'But that's so unfair!' Marina said with a frown. 'Why should the bad Sprites get away with using their magic to hurt people?'

Grandma nodded. 'I know, sweetheart, it does seem unfair. But perhaps some day they will face the consequences.'

'So *did* Glenda have magic powers, too?' asked Flame.

'Yes, Flame – she did,' replied Grandma.

'Wow,' said Flame. 'And did *she* know *you* had magic powers?'

'Yes, we both knew – we could sense it,' said Grandma.

'Did you know if she was one of the bad Sprites?' asked Ash.

'It soon became clear that she was,' replied Grandma.

'So what happened?' asked Flame.

'Well, one night, your grandfather, Sheldon, came to the ballet,' said Grandma. 'I was dancing and I looked out into the audience and saw this young man watching me – and I fell in love with him. I did not know who he was. He saw me dancing on the stage and he fell in love with me. He was so handsome and dashing – that lovely big smile.'

Marilyn Sprite paused for a moment, absorbed in her memory.

The girls watched the dreamy look on her face. They

tried to imagine their grandfather smiling in his theatre seat and their grandmother pirouetting on the stage, with the lights and the music and the audience.

'After the show, your grandfather came backstage and introduced himself to me,' said Grandma. 'He told me his name was Sheldon Sprite. I asked him if he was related to Sidney Sprite – and he said, yes, Sidney was his grandfather. I told him that Sidney's sister was my grandmother and we realised we must be second cousins. We laughed and laughed. He had not realised I was a Sprite when he saw me dancing, as my name was billed on the programme as Marilyn Blackwell – my father's family name. Sheldon asked me to dinner. I accepted, of course. We talked about this amazing family coincidence all the way through our meal.'

'Where did he take you?' asked Marina.

'To a very smart restaurant near the theatre: it was wonderful,' said Grandma. 'He was so charming – such a lovely man. The next day he sent me red roses: every day he sent me roses. He proposed within a month and I agreed to marry him. It was perfect. I was very happy.'

'Then what happened?' asked Flame.

'Well, Glenda was even more jealous,' explained Grandma. 'She thought that your grandfather was smiling at *her* the first night that he came to the ballet. He was not: he was smiling at me, but Glenda said she had seen him first and that he should be her fiancé. But he didn't want to be *her* fiancé: he wanted to be mine! Glenda was furious; she was

56

used to getting her own way – and suddenly she couldn't. When she found out that Sheldon was Sidney Sprite's grandson and owned Sprite Towers – well, that was it! She hit the roof!'

'So, was she a cousin of Grandad, too – like you?' asked Flame.

'Exactly!' replied Grandma. 'We were all three of us second cousins. I had fallen in love with your grandfather without knowing who he was. It was not his money or his house that I wanted – it was him. But Glenda was ambitious – and she wasn't going to let me stand in the way.'

'What did she do?' asked Ash.

'When all this was happening, I was given the star role in the new ballet production,' said Grandma. 'Glenda kicked up a huge stink. She told the manager I would be leaving soon to get married and that she should be given the role, not me.'

'What did they do?' asked Marina.

'The manager took no notice and gave me the role,' said Grandma. 'I was the better dancer.'

'What did Glenda do?' asked Ash.

'Well, strange things started to happen while I was dancing,' said Grandma. 'Instead of being strong and firm as I moved, my legs would suddenly feel like jelly and I would lose my balance. People asked me if I was ill. I said I was fine.

'Then, in a performance one evening, my legs gave way

and I collapsed. The manager sent me home and told me to rest. I was very upset and had to lie in bed for three days. I couldn't move. I thought I might never dance again. The doctors came, but none of them knew what was wrong. Everyone was very worried.

'As I lay there, I thought about what had happened and realised that every time I had felt wobbly, Glenda had been staring at me very intensely. She wanted to ruin my career, but she also wanted me out of the way, so she could try to win over your grandfather.'

'How strong was her magic power, Grandma?' asked Flame.

'She was powerful – and she was angry,' said Grandma. 'People are always more powerful when they are angry, just as they get physically stronger. And, as I told you, Glenda's branch of the family play by different rules.'

'So what did you do?' asked Marina.

'Well, once I realised what was happening, I could heal myself with my mind,' replied Grandma. 'I took time out to rest and regain my balance. I talked to my grandmother and she taught me how to protect myself by shielding myself with my power. While I was away from the ballet, Glenda danced my role, as my understudy – so of course she was not happy to see me back as the prima ballerina. All the time I was near her, I shielded myself against her power, so that I kept my balance.

'I should have left it at that, but I did not. Glenda kept

goading me and said some dreadful things: she was very unkind. I was angry and I started to use my power to make her stumble when she was dancing – tit for tat. She fell over several times during performances and I could see she was furious. Ballerinas are not supposed to fall over.'

'Did Glenda know it was you?' asked Flame.

'Oh yes, she knew it was me!' said Grandma.

'What did the other dancers think?' asked Flame.

'I think they thought Glenda and I had both caught a virus that made us lose our balance,' said Grandma. 'Only Glenda and I knew the truth.'

'Did you tell Grandad what really happened?' asked Marina.

'No, sweetie, I didn't tell him.' Her grandmother smiled and shook her head.

'Why not?' asked Marina.

'Because, as I say, people who do not have magic powers find it difficult to understand,' said Grandma. 'It was better to keep quiet about it.'

'And you *knew* Grandad Sheldon didn't have magic powers?' said Flame.

'That's right,' nodded Grandma.

'Is that what's called "intuition", Grandma?' asked Flame.

'It is, indeed,' said Grandma. 'It's one of the most important abilities we human beings have. There are some things you just know.'

'Did you ever tell your parents about your power?' asked Flame.

'No,' Grandma shook her head. 'I thought they might be cross with me.'

'And would they have been?' asked Flame.

'I don't think that any more,' said Grandma. 'But I did when I was young.'

'Do you wish you *had* told them?' Ariel asked quickly.

'No, sweetheart,' Grandma replied. 'I would have risked losing my power if I didn't keep it secret, remember? And I was lucky that I had my grandmother to talk to – like you do with me.'

'Is it a bad thing to have magic power, Grandma?' asked Ash, frowning.

'No, Ash, it's a wonderful thing to have, providing you always use it wisely,' said Grandma. 'As I grew older, I began to realise that my magic was a very special thing. I would find birds with broken wings or animals that had been hurt. I would hold them and stroke them – their bones mended and they got better.'

'Did you ever use your magic to fight other people, before Glenda?' asked Flame.

'Never,' replied Grandma. 'And when I did use it to hurt her, I knew it was wrong, that it was against the Sprite Code of Honour.'

'So did you lose your powers, Grandma?' asked Ariel.

'Not straight away,' replied Grandma. 'But things got

more serious. I was very upset and frightened. I was worried that Glenda might permanently injure my legs. And she had humiliated me in front of all the other dancers. Your grandfather, Sheldon, was terribly worried: he thought I was ill. Glenda was determined to push me out of the ballet and get your grandfather. She wanted to live at Sprite Towers. I did not know what to do.'

'So how did you stop her?' asked Marina.

'Well, late one night, Glenda followed me out of the theatre,' said Grandma. 'As I walked down a dark, narrow street, she came up behind me. She was very angry and started threatening me. There was nobody about. I was alone – and terrified she was going to hurt me. She raised her finger and pointed it at me – but before she summoned her power she started to laugh.'

'What did you do then?' asked Flame.

'Thankfully, I was quicker than her,' said Grandma. 'I pointed both my hands at her and shouted that I wished she would die.'

'Oh!' the Sprite Sisters looked shocked.

'Yes, it was a dreadful thing to say.'

'Did she die?' asked Ariel.

'No, she didn't die, but she was very ill for many months. By the time she came back to the ballet, your grandfather and I had married and moved away.'

'Did you ever see her again?' asked Marina.

'I haven't seen her for over forty years,' said Grandma.

'She may be a second cousin and the same family, but I have no idea what happened to her. She was a mean, nasty woman. Thankfully, she went out of my life.'

'What happened to your power after that?' asked Marina.

'It went away and I have not felt it since,' said Grandma. She sighed deeply. 'I was unable to mend another bird's wing. I forgot about it until you girls grew up and I knew you were all special. Sometimes now, just sometimes, I think my fingers are tingling, but then the moment passes. Maybe the power is still there, somewhere.'

'Do you think it will come back one day?' asked Marina.

'Who knows?' Grandma looked at her long, slim hands. She touched the gold wedding ring and the huge diamond and ruby engagement ring that Sheldon had given her over forty years ago and she smiled.

'Why do you think your power disappeared so suddenly?' asked Flame.

'I broke the Sprite Code of Honour,' said Grandma. 'My family are good Sprites – and you cannot have good magic powers if you send out horrible thoughts. I should not have reacted in the way I did. I paid the price by losing my power.'

The four Sprite Sisters were silent. Huddled on the bed in the gathering dark, they looked at their grandmother for reassurance.

'So you see, my dears, you must always think before you use your magic,' said Grandma. 'Don't just use it for fun or point a finger or stamp a foot or blink an eye every time you feel annoyed with someone. You must learn to deal with life without using magic against people. Use your power only ever to make something good happen or to protect yourselves.'

The Sprite Sisters thought about this for a moment.

'Were we right to use magic with the slugs?' asked Flame.

'They would have destroyed the vegetable garden if you hadn't got rid of them, and we rely on your father's vegetables to feed us – so, yes, I think so,' said Grandma. 'You did the right thing, Flame.'

Flame smiled, relieved.

'Where did you leave them?' asked Grandma.

'Outside the wall on the grassy track,' replied Flame. 'I burned a circle in the grass around them. We wanted them to stay in one place and not to come back into the garden.'

'Very wise,' said Grandma. 'But they may not stay there for long. What will you do with them then?'

'We're going to check them after school tomorrow, then decide what to do,' said Flame. 'We need to find some- where safe to put them that isn't near the vegetable garden.'

'Right, now it's bedtime,' Grandma smiled. 'That was a lovely musical performance you gave us this evening. You are going to play beautifully at the concert on Friday; I am so proud of you all.'

Flame, Marina and Ash got off Ariel's bed and kissed their grandmother goodnight.

'Sleep well, my darlings.' Grandma hugged them all, then bent down to kiss Ariel on the cheek – but the youngest Sprite Sister was already asleep.

I wonder if she understood what I said about using her magic power wisely, thought Grandma, as she pulled the duvet over Ariel's shoulders. Somehow she did not think so. Her little granddaughter looked like an angel, but she was mischievous.

I shall have to keep a close eye on her, thought Grandma, as she closed the bedroom door.

CHAPTER SIX

CELEBRITY SLUGS

Monday morning was sunny and bright. The Sprite family was eating breakfast when the doorbell rang.

'Who on earth can that be, so early?' said Dad, through a mouthful of scrambled egg.

'I'll get it,' said Flame and she walked through the big hall. She drew back the bolt, turned the huge iron handle and pulled open the front door.

On the doorstep was a man holding a microphone. Behind him was a man with a television camera resting on his shoulder and another man wearing big earphones.

'Good morning!' beamed the microphone man. 'Are

you Miss Sprite? Are your parents here?'

'Good morning,' replied Flame. 'Yes, they are – what's this about?'

'The lesser-snouted thribble-horned slugs that were found just outside your property yesterday!' smiled the man.

Flame gulped. Oh heck, she thought.

'Hold on a moment, please,' she said and pushed the door almost shut.

'Who is it, Flame?' said Dad, walking through the hall-way towards her. He looked through the crack in the door. 'Who are all those people?' he asked.

'It's the television news,' she said. 'Something about the slugs.'

'Slugs?' said Dad. 'Oh Lord!'

Flame rushed through to the kitchen to warn her sisters.

Dad opened the front door.

'Good morning, Mr Sprite!' said the television man. 'I'm Grant Smithers from the local news channel.'

He held up the microphone to Dad's face. Dad pushed it down.

'Good morning, Mr Smithers,' he said. 'What is going on?'

'Mr Sprite, are you aware that a find of national impor-tance was made just outside your property yesterday afternoon?'

'No,' said Dad. Was the man completely mad, he won-dered? How could a load of slugs be of national importance?

'Mr Sprite, I'd like to ask you a few questions,' said Grant Smithers. 'Yesterday afternoon, Dr Phil Lemon, a malacologist from the university discovered a sizeable number of very rare lesser-snouted thribble-horned slugs on a piece of ground just the other side of your garden wall.'

'What?' said Dad. It was the second time in the last twenty-four hours that he had heard the word malacologist. He stared in horror as another van pulled into the driveway of Sprite Towers. A camera flashed and a reporter from the local newspaper hurried forward; behind him was a photographer.

'Mr Sprite, we'd like your comments, please,' continued Grant Smithers, elbowing the reporter out of the way.

'Well . . . er . . . it's wonderful news, of course, that these rare creatures have been found,' said Dad. 'I am delighted.'

'What are your thoughts on the mysterious ring of fire burned around the slugs?' asked Grant Smithers, raising the microphone up to Dad's nose. 'Would you know anything about that?'

'Me?' said Dad. He looked flabbergasted.

'What about your family, Mr Sprite?' persisted Grant Smithers. 'What are their comments?'

Dad drew a deep breath, stood up straight and looked Grant Smithers in the eye. He was not going to stand there on live television and be bullied into talking about his family, especially his daughters.

'Excuse me a minute,' he said. He pushed the microphone aside, went inside and shut the door tight.

Flame was standing in the hall, along with her sisters.

'WHAT is going on?' said Dad.

'I don't know, Dad! Really I don't!' said Flame.

'Where did you put the slugs? What is this ring of fire? Did you go round behind the wall?' Dad spluttered.

'We threw the slugs over the wall, like we told you – and then later we, er, burned a ring on the grass, so the slugs would stay there and not come back into the garden,' said Flame.

Dad looked at his daughters.

'Did you girls go out of the grounds yesterday afternoon?' he asked.

The Sprite Sisters stared at their father – then the doorbell rang again.

Dad spun round and looked at the door. 'What am I going to say?'

'*Say nothing*,' said Grandma, who had walked up behind the Sprite Sisters.

Dad gawped at Grandma.

'What?'

'Say that you are as surprised as anyone else – but you know nothing about the slugs,' said Grandma, very firmly.

'But that's lying – we *do* know about the slugs!' said Dad, flustered.

'*What* do we know?' asked Grandma. 'They were here one minute and gone the next. We have no idea how they got here. The girls told you they threw them out of the garden. Believe me, Colin, it will be much easier if you say we know nothing.'

Dad hesitated, holding the door handle. The Sprite Sisters watched him, tense with anticipation.

'I agree with your mother, Colin,' said Mum, who had joined them. 'We don't know what happened or how the slugs got here – and we don't want to get the girls involved. Besides, there will be people crawling all over the garden for weeks if we say we found them here.'

'Oh Lord, I hadn't thought of that,' said Dad, rubbing his chin. Dad looked from Mum to Grandma and then to the Sprite Sisters.

'We won't say anything Dad!' said Ash, sensing his hesitation.

'Don't tell them, Dad – please!' implored Marina.

Colin Sprite blew out hard. He was an honest man and right now he felt very uncomfortable.

'Okay– we know nothing,' he agreed and slapped his hand on his thigh. 'Not a word to anybody.'

Dad opened the front door. A camera flashed and a microphone was held up to his face. He smiled at the news teams.

'Well, Mr Smithers, I have asked my family about the slugs, but nobody here knows anything about them,' he said. 'We are delighted to know that Dr Lemon has found and identified a rare species, but we are unable to help with your enquiries.'

'What about the ring of fire made around the slugs – have you any comment on that?' Grant Smithers persisted, holding the microphone up to Dad's face again.

'No,' said Dad. 'As you can see, we have a very high wall around Sprite Towers and are rather shut away from the outside world.'

Grant Smithers looked disappointed.

'I'm sorry Mr Smithers, but we don't seem to be of any help,' said Dad. 'Now we really must get the girls to school.'

Dad smiled at Grant Smithers and shut the front door.

A few minutes later, the Sprite Sisters came out of the house. Grant Smithers and the newspaper reporter were still standing on the driveway.

Flame, Marina and Ash smiled politely and walked towards Mum's car.

Ariel waved at the reporter.

It would be so funny to tell him how I used my magic power to whoosh the slugs over the wall, she thought.

Ariel opened her mouth to say something – but Flame saw her and grabbed her arm.

'Don't say a word!' said Flame, through the side of her mouth.

'Ow!' squeaked Ariel.

As they waited for Mum by the car, Flame, Marina and Ash all stood around Ariel, as if guarding a prisoner. Ariel stamped her foot with frustration.

At last, Mum came out of the house, holding her car keys. Grant Smithers walked up to her with the microphone.

'Why don't you drive round and see the place where the slugs were found?' Mum said to him before he could ask her any questions.

'Thank you, Mrs Sprite,' said Grant. 'We have already done that. I'm just mystified about this ring of fire and how it got there – so close to your house. Have you any ideas about it?'

Mum shook her head and smiled sweetly.

'No, I'm afraid not – as my husband said, we are a bit shut away here,' said Mum. 'It's very exciting news, but please excuse me – I must get my daughters to school.'

While all this excitement was going on at Sprite Towers, one mile away, in another big house, a woman with a chignon of pale blond hair was spreading a very thin layer of butter over a very thin piece of toast. She was half watching the television news as she ate her breakfast and looked up with interest as she heard the words 'Sprite Towers'. Grabbing the remote with a perfectly manicured hand, she turned up the volume and stared at the screen.

Grant Smithers was standing in front of Sprite Towers. 'Where these very rare slugs came from, and who burned

71

a ring of fire around them, remains a mystery,' he said. 'The owner of the house, Mr Colin Sprite, says the family knows nothing about the slugs, which were found yesterday by Dr Phil Lemon, a malacologist at the university . . .'

The woman smiled and chewed slowly and very precisely on her piece of toast.

Well, well, well, she thought. I'll bet I know who burned that ring of fire. I'll bet my bottom dollar this has something to do with those dear little Sprite Sisters. Those girls have inherited their grandmother's magic.

The woman stared at the television screen with icy blue eyes and smiled a cold, cold smile.

This is going to be fun, she thought.

CHAPTER SEVEN

FLAME'S 'PING' MOMENT

MUM DROPPED the Sprite Sisters off in the Quad, the huge courtyard at the front of Drysdale's School.

It was an old and famous school with an impressive array of buildings, covered with stone crests showing the school coat of arms. Around the school were huge grounds, with big grass hockey pitches and cricket fields and at the side, a stone chapel with a bell, which was rung every morning for assembly. The pupils wore smart dark navy blazers decorated with yellow braid. At break, the younger boys and girls put on navy-coloured boiler suits, so they could run around and get messy in the woods.

The Sprite Sisters had attended Drysdale's since they were seven years old and they all loved it. They would stay there until they were eighteen. At the moment they were all in the prep school, but in the autumn term Flame would go up to the senior school. Marina would follow her the next year.

As the Sprite Sisters got out of the car that morning, Ash said to Ariel, 'Don't forget what Grandma told us about keeping our magic powers secret.'

'Yeah, yeah,' said Ariel.

'Ariel, this is *really* important!' said Ash. 'It's not funny! And don't say anything to anyone about the slugs!'

'What if they ask me?' said Ariel.

'Just say you don't know anything about them,' said Ash. 'Come on or we'll be late.'

Flame was about to turn around and say something to Ariel too when Quinn walked up to her. He had dark hair and bright, dark eyes and Flame thought he was gorgeous.

'Hi!' he smiled.

'Hi!' Flame blushed. She wished she didn't blush when Quinn spoke to her, but she always did. He was a year older than her and already in the senior school. His sister, Janey, was Marina's best friend, and they lived near Sprite Towers.

'Great party on Saturday night – thanks for that,' said Quinn.

'Yes, it was fun,' said Flame.

'We just saw you on the television,' grinned Quinn.

'Oh,' said Flame.

'You were all standing in the front door and your father was saying he didn't know anything about the slugs that were found outside your wall,' said Quinn.

'I s'pose everyone will have seen it,' said Flame. She bit her lip anxiously.

'Well, it's nothing to worry about!' laughed Quinn. 'Typical of you Sprites – most people *want* to be on the telly, but not you lot, eh!'

Flame smiled.

'Catch you later,' said Quinn and turned to go.

'You too,' said Flame and walked ahead towards the school entrance in a dream, forgetting all about her sisters.

As Marina, Ash and Ariel walked towards the main door of the prep school, the Tolver twins – known collectively as 'Trouble' – bounced up.

'Morning!' they shouted cheerily.

Alex and Bill were twelve years old and looked like peas in a pod with their sandy-coloured hair and blue eyes. Sometimes it was hard to tell them apart. They were rough, tough boys, always untidy and always naughty – and they loved teasing Marina, Ash and Ariel. Flame they were wary of, however.

'Saw you all on the telly this morning!' they laughed.

The Sprite Sisters looked at one another in surprise.

'Funny that all those slugs were *outside* your garden,' said Bill, kicking a small stone with a scuffed shoe.

'Why?' asked Marina.

''Cos we put them *inside* your garden – that's why!' laughed Alex.

'What do you mean you "put them inside our garden"?' asked Marina, standing in front of Bill.

He stopped.

'Well?' she demanded, her hands on her hips.

'We saw these two humungous great orange and black slugs at the wildlife centre some months ago,' Bill laughed. 'We got some of their eggs on a leaf and took them home and put them in a glass aquarium full of leaves and soil. We hid it under Alex's bed. The slugs hatched out and we fed them up – till Mum found out. There were over a hundred of them by then. Mum threw a total wobbly and told us to chuck them out, so we thought we'd throw them over your garden wall!'

The boys hooted with laughter.

'So how come yesterday they were outside your wall and you didn't know anything about them?' said Alex.

'I don't know – they must have climbed over the wall,' said Marina.

'Yeah, right,' said Bill, looking doubtful. 'And who burned the ring of fire?'

'I have no idea,' said Marina. 'But if I were you, I'd

keep very quiet or you might find the police on your doorstep! There are laws about stealing rare slugs!'

She looked so cross that the twins decided to leave it there.

'Okay, okay – keep your hair on,' said Alex, holding up his hands.

'I mean it – keep quiet about this or you'll get in trouble!' said Marina.

'What's *her* problem?' said Bill, kicking another stone – and off they went.

Ash and Marina looked at one another.

'Phew!' they both said.

'Well, at least we know how the slugs got in the garden,' said Ash. 'It will solve one mystery for Dad.'

As Flame hung up her blazer in the cloakroom, her best friend, Pia, came in. Pia was small and graceful like a fawn and had dark eyes and a soft smile. She was patient, which was a good quality to have as Flame's best friend. Flame was not patient; she liked to try new things and often challenged the teachers, asking them difficult questions in class. Where Flame was bold, Pia was calm. The girls had been best friends since they started school. They were both popular, though some girls were wary of Flame's quick temper.

Flame was tense, worried about whether anyone would find out the truth about the slugs. Then Verena Glass walked in.

Flame could feel the hair stand up on the back of her neck. There was something about Verena that really irritated her. Sometimes, it was the way Verena sneered at people; at other times it was because she thought Verena cared about nothing. Either way, the girls did not like each other and even less so recently, since Quinn had become friends with Verena.

'Trying to become TV celebrities now, are we?' sniffed Verena.

Flame flinched and was about to react.

'Don't!' hissed Pia very quietly, touching her arm.

Verena flicked back her long smooth blond hair, threw an icy smile at Pia and walked out of the cloakroom.

By morning break, the story of the Sprite Sisters and the slugs was all around the school. After break, Flame and Pia walked back towards their classroom for a maths lesson. Verena followed them along the corridor, surrounded by her friends.

'You know, it's really very strange that none of you Sprites know anything about these slugs,' said Verena loudly, grinning her cool, superior grin.

Flame spun round.

'Curious how they were just over *your* wall, isn't it?' continued Verena. 'Interesting that a "ring of fire" was put around them, don't you think? Matches, was it? Or could there be another explanation?'

Flame was speechless. She felt her heart pounding. Did Verena know about the Sprite Sisters' magic powers? Surely, she couldn't!

Pia stood at her side.

Flame Sprite and Verena Glass stood half a metre apart, their eyes locked. They were exactly the same height and build. Verena knew exactly how to wind Flame up and she loved every minute of it. She smiled as she saw Flame's face colouring and heard her breathing get faster.

The corridor seemed to go strangely quiet.

Pia looked anxiously at her friend. Usually, Flame reacted quickly and sharply – and Verena knew this. She was waiting for Flame to get angry, while, she, Verena, would stay as cool as a cucumber. Verena was very good at staying cool. Afterwards, she would quite calmly tell the teachers that Flame had provoked a fight – or so she hoped.

But, as if reading her mind, Flame had a sudden intuition that she should not react. She was just about to say something, when she had what her father called a 'ping' moment.

A 'ping' moment is the moment when you realise something really important, and don't do what you were about to do; or, it could be a moment in which you *do* do something that you weren't about to do. Either way, it is a moment of sudden awareness and you do the opposite of what you thought you were going to do.

In a 'ping' moment you always do the right thing, so Dad said.

As Flame Sprite felt the 'ping' in the back of her mind, she knew she should say nothing at all; that she should not attempt to explain away the slugs, nor apologise. She knew she would get into deep water. The Sprite Sisters had used magic to deal with the slug invasion and nobody must find out. Flame instinctively knew she had to be careful.

Everybody waited. Verena raised her left eyebrow and looked questioningly at Flame.

Flame Sprite looked at Verena – and said nothing. Her face was calm, her breathing normal. She suddenly felt terribly grown up. She smiled at Verena, then turned around and walked off down the corridor.

'Phew, Flame!' said Pia, following.

Later on, during the maths lesson, Flame felt Verena watching her on several occasions, and took no notice.

At lunchtime, Flame saw Marina outside the refectory. The two girls moved down the corridor to talk unheard, as Drysdale's pupils walked past.

'I had a run-in with Verena Glass,' said Flame. 'Everybody knows about the slugs and I think they think we are hiding something.'

'The Tolver twins told us they'd thrown the slugs over our garden wall,' said Marina, pulling back her curly dark hair.

'What?' said Flame, turning to face Marina. 'What if they talk?'

'I told them they'd have the police on to them if they said anything,' said Marina.

'Why didn't you put the fear of God into them?'

'I *did*!' Marina retorted. 'But you know how they like a good story.'

'They'll talk!' said Flame, frowning. 'I have no idea how we'll get out of all this.'

'Why are you cross with me?' said Marina, ever sensitive to Flame's temper and suddenly feeling as if this was all her fault.

'I'm not cross with *you*,' said Flame. 'I'm just *cross*. I didn't know what Verena knew or what to say back to her. She's so catty. Sometimes it feels hard having magic powers, always having to hide things from people. I wish I'd been there with the twins – I'd have told them!'

'I *did* tell them!' Marina bristled. 'Why do you always think you're the only one who can sort things out?'

Flame was stung by this remark and was silent.

'It's weird not being able to talk about all this to Mum and Dad,' said Marina, quietly.

'Sure is,' sighed Flame.

'It'll be okay – just as long as no one finds out about our magic,' said Marina.

For a few seconds the two sisters were silent, then Marina said, 'I wonder what would happen if Mum and

Dad found out we used magic on the slugs?'

Flame bit her lip. 'I don't know, but I think we'd better be very careful how we use our powers from now on.'

'Ariel could get us all in a heap of trouble,' said Marina.

'We must watch her like hawks,' agreed Flame.

CHAPTER EIGHT
✳

NEWS AND
A NIGHTMARE
✴ ✴
✴

BY THE time the Sprite Sisters had got back from school on Monday afternoon, the television vans had left. After their music practice – which went well – the Sprite family sat down to supper.

Dad was keen to find out about the girls' part in the slug 'ring of fire'.

Had they done it? And if so, how had they made it? And why? And how had the slugs got into the garden of Sprite Towers in the first place?

There were questions for which Dad wanted answers. But, as usual, he was thwarted.

He was just expressing surprise at the Sprite Sisters' curious lack of interest in the slugs – a new-found national treasure, after all – when Grandma came to their rescue.

'It's a very important week for the girls, Colin. I expect they are thinking about the concert – it's only four days away,' she said.

'Well, maybe . . . but I do think it's all very mysterious,' said Dad, grappling with a piece of broccoli on his plate. 'I sometimes wonder if I shall ever get a straight answer.' Why, wondered Dad, were things always so complicated?

At which point, Ash came to his rescue. 'The Tolver twins put the slugs in our garden, Dad.'

'What? Why?' Dad was aghast.

'They thought it would be funny,' said Ash, biting her lip.

'I'll give them funny, the next time I see them,' fumed Dad, stabbing another piece of broccoli.

'Wouldn't it be fantastic if Drysdale's won the National Schools Music Competition?' Marina quickly interjected.

'Wouldn't it just!' agreed Mum. 'Everyone has worked so hard – but then I expect the other schools have, too.'

'It'll be weird standing up there on the stage playing in front of all those people,' said Ariel. She twiddled her fork on her plate, lost in her own world.

'Yes, it will be a big day for you all – but I'm sure you'll be fine,' smiled Mum. 'Now, would anyone like some more fish pie?'

Flame was quiet at the supper table. She did not tell her family about her run-in at school with Verena Glass that day.

Strangely, Verena came into the conversation in quite another way.

'I got a call today from Stephen Glass on a work matter,' said Dad. 'You know he's Verena's father?'

The girls nodded.

'He's been a bit low: his wife left last week. She's run off with a chap and gone to live in Buenos Aires,' said Dad.

'Oh dear!' said Mum. 'Poor Stephen – and poor Verena!'

'Hmm,' agreed Dad. 'Sad business.'

Flame thought of Verena and what happened that morning. She must have been feeling sad inside that icy shell of hers, Flame thought, and she felt relieved she had not reacted to Verena's attempt to wind her up.

'Who is going to look after Verena?' asked Mum. 'Stephen is only there at weekends – and not many of those.'

'Why is that?' asked Ash.

'He's a lawyer in London,' explained Dad. 'He's got pots of money, but works incredibly long hours. Verena's grandmother has come to live with her – she moved in on Sunday afternoon. Apparently, she's very glamorous and has brought lots of hat boxes!'

'Verena always has amazing holidays and expensive clothes,' said Marina. She loved clothes and sometimes wished her family had more money to spend on things like that.

'Expensive clothes are no substitute for having a happy family life,' said Mum, thoughtfully. 'I hope Verena will be able to go out and see her mother in the school holidays. She must be missing her.'

The Sprite family ate silently for a moment as they thought on this.

'Funny thing is, Verena is a distant cousin of yours, girls,' said Dad.

'What?' the Sprite Sisters chorused. 'How?'

Flame was horrified. 'Verena Glass and I are related? I don't believe you!'

'Well, only a very distant cousin: Stephen Glass's great-uncle was Sidney Sprite,' said Dad. 'His great-grandmother was one of Sidney's sisters. We're a big family – there are Sprites everywhere.'

The Sprite Sisters looked at one another in astonishment.

'Why didn't you tell ever us about Verena before, Dad?' demanded Flame.

'Never really thought about it before,' he replied, surprised at her reaction. 'I don't spend much time thinking about family trees, interesting though I am sure they are – and none of you has shown any interest before. Why, have you some objection to Verena?'

'You know Verena and I hate each other!' said Flame. She placed her knife and fork together on her plate. This news was too much. She stood up and looked at Mum. 'Excuse me, Mum, but I don't want any pudding this evening,' said Flame. 'Do you mind if I get down? I'm really tired and I'd like to get an early night.'

Mum looked up anxiously at her eldest daughter.

'That's fine, love,' she said. 'Listen, don't start getting too wound up about this concert, will you? It's only a concert, Flame – remember that. I know you want Drysdale's to win – but think of it as fun, eh? And don't worry about the slug fiasco.'

'Yes – thanks, Mum. Night everyone.' Flame kissed her mother and waved a hand at the rest of the family.

Mum sighed. This wasn't the first time Flame had left the table when she was feeling uptight. She knew her daughter felt things very intensely and liked to be alone to sort things out in her head.

'She'll be fine, Ottalie – she just needs to rest,' Grandma said to Mum, then she diverted the conversation again, asking Dad, 'Which grandmother has come to look after Verena, Colin?'

'Stephen's mother,' replied Dad. 'I've never met her. She's lived abroad for years. I understand she's been married several times. Now she's called Mrs Glass again – although I think that might have been her second husband's name.'

Grandma shivered. A sudden chill went down her back. She felt icy cold, despite the warmth of the kitchen.

'Are you all right, Marilyn?' asked Mum. 'You look very pale.'

The Sprite family looked her anxiously.

'You're shivering,' said Mum, getting up from the table.

'I'm fine, thank you,' said Grandma.

'Let's put something round your shoulders,' said Mum, reaching for the shawl that always hung over the back of the Windsor chair.

For a moment, Grandma shut her eyes. As she opened them, the colour started to return to her cheeks.

The family smiled with relief.

'It was just a little turn – nothing to worry about. Thank you, dear,' she said to Mum, as she drew the shawl around her.

What was it about hearing about Verena's grandmother that upset her, she wondered? Sidney Sprite had three sisters – there were distant cousins all over the place. The Sprites were a big family, as Dad had said.

Grandma did not know for sure what, but something had made her feel fearful. It was the same feeling as she'd had Sunday afternoon, when they were all sitting outside in the sunshine and the sky seemed to go dark for an instant.

Marina, Ash and Ariel gave their grandmother an especially big hug as they said goodnight that evening. They loved her dearly and were frightened when she looked ill.

Upstairs, on the second floor of the house, Flame turned out her bedroom light. If anyone looked in, she would pretend to be asleep.

She felt confused. On the one hand, she was happy – she'd had a wonderful birthday party and was about to play in the concert. On the other hand, she was worried that she and her sisters could be exposed for having magical powers. And she hated the fact that Mum and Dad had needed to lie to the television man about the slugs. They never told fibs – and Flame knew this would weigh on them.

Added to this, she was upset about her clash at school with Verena Glass and the awful news that she and Verena were distant cousins. It was all so strange.

There was a lot to think about. And, right at the back of Flame's mind, there was something else niggling – but she couldn't work out what it was.

She gave a long sigh and fell into a deep sleep.

The curtains opened. The lights blazed.

'Ladies and gentlemen, it is with great pleasure that I introduce to you the fabulous, the fantastic, the phantas-magorical Sprite Sisters!' boomed Mr Taylor, Drysdale's School's head of music through the microphone, waving his right arm with an extravagant flourish towards the girls.

Flame, Marina, Ash and Ariel Sprite smiled and bowed.

The audience clapped and clapped.

Here they were, high up on the stage, underneath the bright stage lights on their big night – the first time they had ever played together in public.

Flame looked at her sisters. Their faces were flushed with excitement.

Flame gripped her violin and sat poised, ready to play. Marina stretched out her bow arm and held her viola under her chin. Ash leaned in towards her cello and Ariel brought her flute up to her mouth, ready to blow. Their practice had been perfect. The stage was set. The audience waited.

Marina, Ash and Ariel looked at Flame. 'One, two, three,' she counted briskly, and off they went into a folk song they had rehearsed together a hundred times this last month.

It started beautifully, but three bars into the music, something went horribly wrong. Instead of a pretty little folk song, there was a screeching of violin. One of Ash's cello strings snapped and flew into the air with a loud twang; Marina's viola let out an ear-piercing screech; Ariel's flute made a horrible rasping sound and Flame found she had no strength in her arm to draw the bow properly across her violin. All she could do was squeak. The noise was ghastly!

The Sprite Sisters stopped playing and looked at each other in horror.

Flame looked out at the audience. Mum, Dad and

Grandma were standing up by their seats in disbelief.

Whatever is happening? they wondered.

The headmaster and his wife, sitting in the front row, were open-mouthed in astonishment. The five hundred people watching the concert sat amazed at the awful noise.

Then Flame saw a face in the audience that made her blood run cold. A woman about the same age as her grandmother was roaring with laughter and pointing her finger at the Sprite Sisters. She had a chignon of pale blond hair swept back on to the nape of her neck and beautifully manicured nails.

The woman's eyes were cold, so cold.

Flame felt the sensation of panic. She could not breathe.

'No!' she shouted out. 'No! Stop! It's not meant to be like this! Something has happened!'

Then everything went dark.

Flame woke suddenly with a big jolt.

She was dripping with sweat and panting heavily as Marina opened the bedroom door and said softly, 'Flame, are you all right? You were shouting.'

Flame could not answer. She gasped for breath.

'Here, sit up, sis,' said Marina, gently pulling Flame into a sitting position. Then she sat down on the bed and took her sister's hand.

'It's okay,' said Marina, softly stroking Flame's hair.

'You were having a nightmare, but it's all over now.'

Flame nodded, but could not speak. She could hear Marina talking, but all she could see was the face of the woman.

'It's all gone now,' said Marina.

Flame gave a long sigh.

The bedroom door opened again. Ash walked to the bed and sat down beside Marina.

'I heard you shouting! What were you dreaming about?' she asked.

'We were playing at the concert,' whispered Flame. 'Something went wrong and I couldn't work out what it was. It was awful, we made the most dreadful sound. There were all these people watching – and there was this horrible woman laughing at us. I knew that somehow she'd made everything go wrong, that she'd done something to spoil our performance – but I couldn't stop her. She seemed so pleased – and I didn't know what to do.'

Flame began to sob.

'You're just nervous about getting it all perfect,' said Ash, ever practical. 'You know how tense you get before a performance. It'll be fine on the night – you'll see.'

'What's happening?' asked a small voice. Ariel came into the room and climbed on to Flame's bed.

The Sprite Sisters huddled together in the dark and Flame told Ariel about her dream.

'Let's hold hands like we did the other day and see if we

can make that blue circle of light,' suggested Ariel. 'It made us all feel happy.'

Flame looked up and smiled. She held out her hands and took Marina's on her left and Ariel's on her right. Opposite her, Ash took Ariel and Marina's hands.

'East, south, west and north,' said Flame. 'Our powers are balanced.'

As the Sprite Sisters held hands, a small blue light began to flicker, as if moving through their arms and bodies. The light grew stronger and stronger until it was a deep, bright blue, surging through them.

'It feels very powerful when we do this,' said Marina.

'Yes, it does,' agreed Flame.

'It's so pretty!' said Ariel.

The Sprite Sisters held the Circle of Power for a few minutes, then they let go of each others' hands. The blue light faded out.

'What do you think it means?' Ash asked her sisters.

'I don't know – but it's something to do with the way we use our magic powers together,' said Flame.

'I think it means we're going to play magnificently on Friday!' Marina said to Flame. 'Ash is right – it'll be fine on the night. No more worrying, Flame: settle down and get some rest.'

They all gave their sister a hug, then Flame rolled over in her bed, pulled up the duvet cover and shut her eyes.

'Thank you,' she murmured.

The three younger Sprite Sisters waited until their big sister sighed peacefully, then they hugged each other and all went back to bed.

CHAPTER NINE

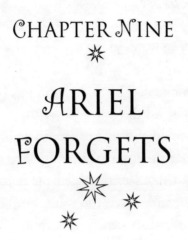

ARIEL FORGETS

TUESDAY TURNED out to be an odd kind of a day.

Flame felt tired as she got up, after the previous night's nightmare. To make things worse, she noticed she had a blemish on her chin: her first spot.

Mum noticed she was pale, kept silent about the spot, but asked her if she was feeling all right. Flame told her she hadn't slept well, but said nothing about the nightmare.

Before breakfast, Marina and Ash ran down the garden to see to the rabbits and guinea pigs. On summer days, the animals lived in long wire cages on the grass. Each day, the girls gave them fresh water and moved the cages around the lawn so the animals had fresh grass to nibble.

Flame was in the dining room, sorting out the music for Friday's concert.

Meanwhile, in the utility room beside the kitchen, Ariel had just put clean water in the hamster cage and was about to open the door of the gerbil cage.

Hamsters move sleepily in the morning, being nocturnal animals. Gerbils, on the other hand, are lively in the day-time: they move quickly and can jump high.

Ariel opened the door of the big wire cage and lifted out the small dish that contained the gerbils' sunflower seeds. Then she unhooked the water bottle on the side of the cage. She was in a dream that morning, as she often was, thinking about her new-found magic powers and about dressing up as a ballerina.

There were two gerbils in the cage, or there were when Ariel opened the door; two small, furry animals with long tails, named Bubble and Squeak. Ariel turned to fill the water bottle at the tap, but forgot to close the cage door. Then she leaned into the cage, fixed the bottle back on the wire and locked the door. All the time, she hummed away happily.

Then Ariel looked closely at the cage: there was something very strange about it.

'EEEH!' she screamed.

Mum rushed into the utility room. 'Whatever is the matter?' she said.

Ariel was waving her arms and sobbing. 'They've gone! The gerbils – they've escaped!'

Frantically, Mum looked round the utility room. Grandma rushed in.

'What's the matter?' asked Grandma.

'Shut the door!' shouted Mum. 'Shut the window! The gerbils have got out!'

Ariel stood in the middle of the room, sobbing, as Flame came in.

'They'll die,' she wailed.

Grandma, Mum and Flame looked behind the washing machine and the freezer; they looked behind the laundry basket and the boxes of detergent. They searched behind the tumble dryer. They caught glimpses of the gerbils now and then, but the little animals were elusive and moved too quickly to catch.

'There's one!' shouted Flame, lunging at Bubble.

'He's over here now!' said Grandma, as Bubble skidded over her foot.

'Mind, you'll stand on him!' said Mum.

It was pandemonium as Dad came in.

'Whatever is going on?' he asked, standing in the open doorway. In front of him was a group of red-faced females, one of them wailing hysterically. And as he stood there, the gerbils made their escape right past his feet.

'Dad, you stupid thing!' shouted Flame, pushing past him.

Colin Sprite looked bewildered. 'What did I do?' he asked, but nobody was interested. Ariel, Mum and Grandma pushed past him to follow the gerbils.

'Oh, Colin – really!' said Mum.

'What?' said Dad again. 'Now what's going on?'

Dad watched as the Sprite women rushed through the kitchen and out into the hall. Sometimes, he thought, it was very hard to understand his family.

The gerbils raced through the kitchen. Pudding, the cat, sprang from the Windsor chair and gave chase.

Ariel screamed again. 'Pudding is going to eat them!' she cried.

Flame followed the gerbils through the hallway and into the drawing-room – and then lost sight of them as they raced under the sofa. She started to push the sofa sideways, when the gerbils ran out from underneath and headed towards the corner of the drawing-room.

Then one disappeared. Flame dived at the other and nearly had hold of it as it followed the first gerbil through a hole in the floorboards – but it was too small and too slippery to grab.

The gerbils made their escape where the radiator pipes went under the drawing-room floor, into a hole just big enough for them to squeeze through.

Marina and Ash came in from the garden to find everyone standing in the drawing-room, staring at the radiator. Ariel was still sobbing: Mum was holding her.

'What's happened?' they asked.

'The gerbils have escaped,' said Flame.

'How?' asked Ash.

'Ariel forgot to shut the cage door when she was feeding them,' said Flame.

Ariel wailed again.

'It'll be all right,' Mum said, soothingly. 'We'll find them – don't worry. Come on, there's nothing we can do now – we must have breakfast.'

The Sprite family looked a sorry lot at the breakfast table that morning. Ariel refused to eat much, which worried Mum. The other sisters munched quietly through bowls of cereal and pieces of toast.

'We'll find them,' said Marina.

'Yes, we will!' said Ash.

Ariel looked reassured.

'Of course, it's possible they could go all over the house, under the floorboards . . .' mused Dad, buttering a piece of toast.

'How, Dad?' asked Flame.

Mum gave her husband a look which said, 'Now you've done it.'

'What do you mean, Dad?' asked Ash.

'Well, they can run around the whole length and width of the house under the floorboards,' he replied. 'They'll run up and along the pipes.'

'They might not know where to come up,' said Marina. 'They could be stuck there for ever. They'll die and we'll never know!'

She started to cry, then Ariel started to cry and Ash sniffed a bit. Flame looked sad.

Dad wished he had not said anything.

'Right, girls, get your bags,' said Mum. 'We're running very late.'

The Sprite Sisters arrived late for school that morning, all looking distracted.

Ariel felt miserable all day, thinking about her gerbils.

Things got worse, however, in the last lesson of the afternoon – history with Mrs Crump.

Ariel wanted to go home. She stared out of the window and watched the clouds. She liked the way they whooshed across the sky.

'Ariel, what do *you* think?' asked Mrs Crump, walking up to her desk.

Ariel spun round on her old wooden chair. She did not know what she thought. She hadn't been listening. What should she say?

'I don't know.' She blinked at Mrs Crump.

'That might be because you did not hear the question,' said Mrs Crump. 'You were too busy looking out of the window.'

Everybody laughed. There was no fooling Mrs Crump.

'We are talking about the Magna Carta, Ariel. Please attend,' said Mrs Crump.

Ariel stared at the history teacher. She liked history because it had lots of stories. But today, she was distracted. If Mrs Crump knew what had happened to her gerbils, thought Ariel, she would not be horrid to her.

But Mrs Crump did not know about the gerbils – and besides, Ariel Sprite often looked out of the window.

Ariel sat up and tried to listen to Mrs Crump, who was talking on and on. She tried to concentrate, but she was bored and worried.

She stared at the teacher, who had a swirly brown bun on the top of her head and dangly, orange earrings. She wore a bright green dress and a pair of bright red spectacles. Ariel thought she looked a bit like a traffic light.

When Mrs Crump read things out to the class, she put on her spectacles. When she looked at the children or wrote on the blackboard, she took them off, and then the spectacles hung around her neck on a thin gold chain.

Ariel looked at the bright red spectacles, which were now sitting on Mrs Crump's ample bosom, then looked around at the other pupils. They were all looking at Mrs Crump. The teacher was waving a hand and talking loudly at the front of the class.

Ariel was sitting at the back of the classroom in the corner beside the window. There was no one behind her or to her left side. In her left hand, she held a pencil. She looked at its pointy lead tip, made a little circle in the air with it, then another.

She looked around again. Her classmates all seemed to be looking at the teacher.

She liked Mrs Crump, but she suddenly had a giggly feeling inside. Given the choice between being good or being naughty, Ariel Sprite always chose naughty.

It was much more fun to be naughty, she thought – not that she set out to hurt anybody. And it was nearly two whole days since Grandma had warned Ariel not to play with her magic powers for fun and she had forgotten.

Maybe I'll have a little go, thought Ariel. Just a teensy go. She pointed the finger holding the pencil and directed it at the spectacles.

Mrs Crump looked down and flinched: she thought she had seen her spectacles lift off her chest. As she looked down, however, Ariel lowered her finger and the red spectacles rested on Mrs Crump's bosom.

Mrs Crump started talking again. Ariel lifted the pencil an eensy bit – and, for a fraction of a second, the red spectacles lifted up again.

The class began to stir. They had noticed something, too.

Mrs Crump looked down at the spectacles again. She could have sworn they had moved.

It is the end of the afternoon, she thought, and my eyes are tired.

She was about to pick up her spectacles and put them

on, so she could write on the board, when Ariel lifted her pencil again.

This time the red spectacles floated up in the air in front of Mrs Crump – and stayed there.

'Argghh!' screamed Mrs Crump.

'Argghh!' went the class and jumped up from their seats.

Ariel lowered her pencil immediately and looked around to check if anybody had spotted her.

Everybody was looking at poor Mrs Crump, who had grabbed her forehead with one hand and the desk with the other – and collapsed on to the desk.

'Did you see that? What was that? What happened?' the class said to one another. Everybody started to shout with excitement.

The classroom door burst open and Batty Blenkinsop, the headmaster, rushed in.

'Mrs Crump! Whatever has happened?'

Ariel giggled. This was much more fun than the Magna Carta, she thought.

'Class – quiet! Sit down, please!' bellowed Batty.

The children settled in their seats, but continued to whisper as Mrs Crump slowly sat up.

'Now will someone tell me what happened?' Batty demanded. It was clear to him that Mrs Crump was in no condition to speak.

Twenty girls and boys – the whole class, except Ariel – spoke at once.

'Her spectacles floated!'

'Her glasses lifted up!'

'She's got magic glasses!'

'Mrs Crump fainted!'

'Okay, thank you – that's enough!' said Batty. The children were talking gibberish, he thought. Floating spectacles – huh!

'Monica, I am leaving you in charge for a few minutes while I take Mrs Crump to Nurse,' he said to the bossiest girl in the glass, as Mrs Crump slowly came round.

Monica walked to the front and looked at her classmates, while Batty took Mrs Crump by the arm and led her out of the classroom.

Then the entire class burst out laughing and shouting. Nobody took any notice of Monica.

Ariel smiled and laughed too: she thought it was very funny. Nobody seemed to have any idea that she had used her magic power to lift Mrs Crump's spectacles.

Five minutes later, Batty Blenkinsop reappeared and stood in front of the class. He looked very cross and told everyone to calm down, but he was cut off by the bell for home time.

Mum noticed Ariel was smiling when she greeted her at the school gate.

'Good day, love?' she asked.

'Hmm,' nodded Ariel. 'Mrs Crump's spectacles floated

in the air and she fainted. Mr Blenkinsop came in and took her to Nurse.'

'Oh dear! Poor Mrs Crump!' said Mum, looking down at her small, angelic-looking daughter. 'How on earth did her spectacles float in the air?'

'I don't know,' said Ariel. 'It was funny. Is there any more chocolate cake at home? I'm hungry.'

'Yes, there's lots of chocolate cake.'

'Have you seen the gerbils?' asked Ariel.

'No, not yet – but they'll be back soon,' said Mum, slightly bewildered, as Ash, Marina and Flame approached.

There was a tense silence in the car as Mum drove home.

Flame, Marina and Ash had heard about Mrs Crump's floating spectacles: the story spread around the school like wild fire. Ariel's sisters knew immediately who was responsible, and they were angry. Grandma had told them not to play with their magic only two nights ago. How could Ariel have forgotten already?

To make things worse, Ariel peered at Flame's face and said, 'You've got a spot on your chin.'

That did it. Flame was seething: even Ariel dare not speak after that.

As soon as they entered the front door of Sprite Towers, Ariel, Ash and Marina went to the drawing-room – but there were no gerbils to be seen.

Flame disappeared upstairs to examine the spot.

The sisters said little as they ate their chocolate cake in the kitchen. Ariel knew they were cross with her. Grandma was quiet, too.

Mum watched her daughters and mother-in-law, but could not work out what was happening. She could tell that the older girls were angry with Ariel, and wondered why. Distraction, she decided, would be the best thing, and suggested they all go out to play in the garden before they did their music practice.

The Sprite Sisters ran over the big lawn.

'We need to talk,' said Flame. She said it so strongly that her sisters sat down beside her on the grass under the big beech tree and waited for her to speak.

'Ariel, why on earth did you do that thing with Mrs Crump's spectacles?' asked Flame.

'I thought it was funny,' said Ariel.

'Well, it might have been "funny", but did it occur to you, for one minute, that you could have exposed us all by using your magic powers in public?' Flame was furious.

Ariel's eyes widened. She looked at Ash for support – but Ash, too, looked stern.

'It's serious, Ariel,' she said. 'Flame is right.'

Ariel looked down at the ground.

'I'm sorry,' she whimpered.

'It's not enough to just be sorry,' continued Flame. 'Do you remember what Grandma told us the other night

106

about not playing about with our magic powers?'

'I forgot,' sniffed Ariel.

'Why do you *always* forget things?' shouted Flame.

'I don't know,' Ariel whimpered again, clutching her arms around her knees.

'Do you want to lose your magic power?' said Flame.

'No!' said Ariel, upset.

'Did you understand what Grandma told us – do you remember?' said Flame.

Ariel stared at her elder sister, wide-eyed.

Flame drew a long, deep breath, then said in a deliberate voice. 'She said that we risk losing our power if it is publicly exposed while we are young – that's what she said. Do you want to keep your magic power?'

'Yes,' replied Ariel in a small voice. 'I'm sorry, Flame. I don't think anybody saw me.'

The Sprite Sisters were silent for a minute. Marina stroked Bert's ears as he sat beside her on the grass.

'Flame, you're very tired,' she said. 'I think we've all got the message.'

Flame sighed, heavily. 'There's something else we need to be aware of,' she said.

'What's that?' asked Marina.

Flame looked at each of her sisters; her voice sounded thoughtful and serious. 'I think we are in danger.'

'Danger?' asked Marina. 'What sort of danger?'

Ash and Ariel sat up and stared at their elder sister.

'At the moment, it's just a sense of something I have – but I can't see it clearly,' said Flame.

'What is it you are worried about?' asked Marina, looking into her older sister's eyes. 'Can you see anything at all?'

'I have the sense that there is someone close by who wants to do us harm,' said Flame, quietly.

Marina, Ash and Ariel all drew a sharp breath and looked at one another, anxiously.

'Who would want to hurt us?' said Ash. 'We're just four young girls.'

'Is this something to do with your nightmare?' asked Marina.

Flame nodded. 'I keep getting this feeling that something will happen at the concert. It's hazy at the moment – I will have to wait until I see it more clearly in my mind. I'll tell you as soon as I do.'

'Danger . . .' said Marina quietly, pushing back her dark curly hair from her face. 'It's difficult to think about danger here.'

The Sprite Sisters looked around them, at the lovely garden and the huge house. In a short while, they would sit around the kitchen table with Mum and Dad and Grandma and all laugh together. Right now, their lives did not feel in danger. They were just four girls lolling on the grass in the afternoon sunshine.

'What a week!' said Marina, keen to lighten their

mood. 'Since Saturday we've had the party, the slug attack, television cameras, floating spectacles, Flame's nightmare, possible danger at our concert, missing gerbils – and it's still only Tuesday!'

Hearing the words 'missing gerbils', Ariel sniffed loudly. 'It's all my fault,' she said. 'I wish I hadn't let Bubble and Squeak escape.'

Huge teardrops rolled down her face. She did not have little tears like other people. Ariel's tears sprouted in fat drops, in an instant, but still she managed to look like a sad angel.

'Come on, get a grip, Ariel,' said Flame, half joking. She knew Ariel's ability to divert people's attention away from things when she'd been naughty. 'Losing the gerbils was not as serious as making Mrs Crump's spectacles float, nor as worrying as putting your sisters in danger by exposing your magic power – but it *was* careless,' added Flame.

Ariel bit her lip and looked at the grass. Her tears disappeared as quickly as they had come. She looked round at Ash, who grinned at her.

'What shall we do about the gerbils?' asked Ash.

'How can we use our powers to find them?' said Marina. 'Secretly, of course,' she added quickly.

The Sprite Sisters thought about this for a moment.

'Ash, you could use your power to sense where they are,' said Flame.

'I'll have a go later,' agreed Ash. 'Maybe Ariel could try, too.'

Ariel held up her hands and looked at her pink stubby fingers. 'Could I? But if I find them under the floorboards and make them float up, they might hit their heads.'

'You might be able to blow them along, by making a wind,' suggested Marina.

'Can I do that?' asked Ariel.

'That's part of your magic – harnessing the power of Air,' said Marina.

'We'll put out some food and water near the hole they went through – they might smell it and come up,' said Ash.

'Right,' agreed Flame.

'What about Pudding?' asked Marina.

'We must keep the drawing-room door closed,' said Flame.

'Come on, let's have a swing before tea,' said Ash, jumping up and running off.

And for the next half hour, the Sprite Sisters swung on the huge tractor tyres that hung from the lime tree.

Then they went inside. Ash and Ariel placed two small bowls beside the hole in the drawing-room floor. One contained water and the other sunflower seeds, the gerbils' favourite food. Then, making sure there were no grown-ups about, the two sisters began to hunt for the animals, running their hands over the floorboards and using their magic powers – but neither could sense them.

'We *will* find them,' said Ash to Ariel.

They shut the drawing-room door and hung a 'Keep Shut' notice on the handle.

That evening, the girls' music practice went well and everyone looked more relaxed.

Afterwards, Flame went up to bed for an early night.

Grandma tucked up Ariel and sat down on her bed.

'Are you remembering to keep your magic a secret, Ariel?' she asked gently.

Ariel looked into her grandmother's kind eyes and knew she couldn't lie.

'I'm sorry, Grandma,' said Ariel. 'I promise I'll try harder.'

Grandma stroked Ariel's soft blond hair and looked at her lovely grey eyes. 'I know you will, love,' she said and kissed her goodnight.

Mum came in and kissed her, too. 'We will find the gerbils, won't we?' asked Ariel.

'We'll find them,' said Mum. 'Sweet dreams.'

Ariel was soon asleep, dreaming of being a famous ballerina.

As darkness settled over Sprite Towers, Flame closed her eyes and hoped for peaceful sleep.

CHAPTER TEN

STRANGE HAPPENINGS

ASH WOKE early on Wednesday morning and went to wake Ariel. They planned to search for the gerbils again before school.

Starting in the cellar, the two sisters made their way up through the house: the ground floor, the first floor, the second floor where the girls' bedrooms were – and finally the attics.

The attics were reached by two sets of narrow stairs, one at either end of the second floor of the house. When Sidney Sprite built Sprite Towers, the attics were where the servants slept. These rooms were less grand than the rest of the house; the walls were bare and painted cream. In places you could see patches of damp coming through the ceiling, where one of the roof tiles had slipped and left a hole in the roof.

Sprite Towers' roof was one of Dad's biggest headaches. There were days when he would put his head in his hands and say the family could no longer afford to live there as the house cost too much to keep in good order. But somehow they always found a way through. This was partly because Dad was an architect and clever at mending things. It was also because he and Mum and Grandma rarely sat down. There were always things to do at Sprite Towers and the girls were expected to do their bit.

The Sprite Sisters loved the attics. On rainy days they played hide and seek through the warren of rooms. At either end of the main corridor were the spiral staircases that led up to Sidney Sprite's towers. Going up to the towers was the best treat of all.

That Wednesday, as Ash and Ariel hunted for the gerbils, they ran through the dressing up room, which had dozens of old trunks full of ballgowns, old suits and coats, uniforms with big, brass decorations pinned to them, wonderful hats and long feather boas. Mum said some of these clothes must have been here since the house was built. Each generation of Sprites had added to the boxes of clothes. You could dress up as whatever you wanted: a 1920s flapper, a 1960s chick, a king for a Christmas play, a soldier, a film star or the front end of a donkey: it was all there.

The sisters ran through the train room, which had a huge table covered with a tiny railway track weaving in and out and round it. All over the table, around the tracks, were model houses, trees, little people and tiny animals. The Sprite Sisters thought it was wonderful. Dad loved it too – he had played with it as a boy for hours on end.

As Ash and Ariel ran from room to room, they stopped, stood still and put their hands out over the floor, as if scanning the space beneath them. In the last room – a room full of old paintings stacked up against the walls – Ash stood very still. She got down on her hands and knees and put her hands on the bare floorboards.

'The gerbils are under here,' she said. 'I can feel them.'

Ariel got down and did the same thing. 'I can, too,' she said.

'I can't believe they've come right up to the top of the house,' said Ash. 'We must find them quickly, in case there are any rats about.'

'Rats?' squeaked Ariel.

'Yes, there are always rats close by, wherever you are,' said Ash. 'Dad told me that.'

Ash sat up and thought for a minute. She was very practical and always had good ideas.

'I think we should put a bowl of food on the floor, here, in this room. The gerbils will smell it and come up. I'll put some magic around it – so that when they approach it, they'll be bound to the floor and can't run off. I've never tried using my magic power like this before, but I think it will work. We can check on them as soon as we're home from school. They should be fine.'

Five minutes later, a bowl of sunflower seeds was placed on the floorboards in the attic room; Ash held her hands out flat against the floor and made a magic circle around it using her special Earth power.

Then they ran downstairs to have breakfast.

When Mum dropped off the Sprite Sisters at school that morning, Marina stopped to speak with her friend Janey. Of all the Sprite Sisters, Marina was the one who was most likely to be late. This was because she stopped to talk to people and forgot about the time and where she was going. Janey was equally chatty and the two of them rabbited on for ages.

The Quad was almost empty – everyone had gone to assembly – when Marina and Janey realised they were late. As they made their way across the tarmac, a large silver car pulled in.

It was Verena Glass. Verena was always the last person to arrive at Drysdale's in the morning.

Marina stopped talking and watched the car. She could see the profile of the driver: a woman with sharp features and blond hair swept back off her face. Verena and the woman did not kiss each other goodbye as Verena got out, which Marina thought was strange. The Sprite family always kissed each other hello and goodbye.

Instead, the woman turned her face towards Marina – and stared.

'Why is that woman staring at us like that?' said Janey. 'She looks really cross.'

Marina was a confident girl and easy with people. She had no enemies – and had no reason to expect any. So she looked at the woman with a sense of curiosity, rather than unease.

'I don't know,' replied Marina. 'But I think she's staring at me, not you.'

'Who is she?' asked Janey.

'She must be Verena's grandmother – Dad was telling us about her,' replied Marina.

'Come on, we're ever so late,' said Janey, tugging Marina's arm.

The two girls turned and started to run towards the assembly hall.

As she ran off, Marina felt the woman's eyes on her back. A sensation like an icy shiver passed through her body. The feeling stayed with her for hours.

It was well known at Drysdale's that Verena Glass did everything effortlessly. She always arrived late, but the teachers did not tell her off. She got top marks for her work, without seeming to do any. She was brilliant at sport, without ever seeming to practise.

Verena was always in the right place at the right time – ready to answer the teacher's question, shoot for goal, drive a volley over the tennis net or be chosen for the star part in plays. She also had a beautiful voice and was a renowned singer. Verena made everything look so easy – and she did not seem to care whether or not she came first in everything.

But, while Verena's heart seemed to be icy cold, no one would ever be in any doubt what was in Flame Sprite's heart.

Flame cared passionately and put every bit of effort into everything she did. She tried hard: she was punctual, conscientious and careful. She felt strongly about things – and she stood up and said so.

Every afternoon at Drysdale's, the whole school played sport. On Wednesdays, the younger girls played rounders and the boys played cricket.

Today, as usual, Verena Glass and Flame Sprite were captains of the two rounders teams. Anyone looking at them would see that the two girls were the same height and had the same long legs and arms. They had the same thick hair, the same straight nose and they moved in the same graceful way. The two girls were matched in intelligence, talent and sporting ability – but they would have denied it if anyone pointed it out. At every twist and turn they competed.

It was a hot afternoon and the two rounders teams fought a bitter battle. In the end, Verena's team won.

Flame walked off the field, hot, sweaty and needing a drink of water; Verena looked cool and unruffled.

As Flame passed by her, she called: 'Write yourself a note, Flame, saying, *MUST TRY HARDER*.'

Flame rubbed the back of her arm over her forehead, gritted her teeth and kept walking.

There were times, she thought to herself, when she really hated Verena Glass.

As soon as the Sprite Sisters got home from school, Ash and Ariel raced up to the attics.

'We've got one!' said Ash, as they came through the door of the end room. Sure enough, Bubble the gerbil was sitting, immobilised, on the floorboards. Ash picked him up and gave him to Ariel.

'The magic worked,' said Ash. 'One down, one to go.'

'Thanks, Ash,' said Ariel, smiling.

Ash got down on the floor and put her hands on the boards. 'I don't think Squeak is here – I can't feel him. Let's go and put Bubble back in the cage.' She stood up. 'I think we'd better take this food down – don't want to attract any rats,' she said, and the sisters went downstairs.

It was a warm afternoon, so the Sprite family had tea on the terrace. Dad was working in his office at home and came through to join them. Grandma had baked one of her fruitcakes full of raisins, cherries and nuts. It was one of the Sprite Sisters' favourites and they all had a big piece.

Everyone was pleased that Bubble had been restored to his cage.

'Well done,' said Dad. 'I can't believe the gerbils would go right up there. Which room was it?'

'The end room at the south side,' said Ash. 'By the way, it smelled very damp up there.'

Dad sighed. 'The roof – the roof . . . ah, what shall we do about the roof?'

He stared up at the house.

'Sprite Towers is the only place we want to live, but I have no idea how we will afford to maintain the house,' he said. 'I'm an architect and I can see exactly what needs doing, but there's not enough money to mend the roof while we are committed to four sets of school fees. I will have to make a push for some new contracts.'

Dad swigged a mouthful of tea and sighed again.

Mum and Grandma looked up the house – and they sighed, too.

'Things wouldn't be so tricky if that dratted lawyer hadn't run off with our money when your father died,' said Grandma, looking at her son. 'We were rich then: I could have easily paid for the roof.'

Dad smiled sadly at her.

'Yes, that was a real blow,' he agreed.

'Perhaps the police will catch the lawyer, Grandma,' said Flame.

'Well, you never know,' said Dad. 'They might.'

'And I'm keeping a close eye on my investments,' said Grandma. Since she'd lost her money, Grandma had taken up investing online: she had a sharp eye for a good company and checked the stock market several times a day.

'I saw Verena's grandmother this morning,' said Marina, suddenly.

Everyone looked at her.

'She drove Verena to school – Verena was late, as usual,' said Marina.

'What were *you* doing in the Quad at that time?' asked Mum.

'Talking to Janey,' grinned Marina.

Mum made a face at her as if to say, 'Well, don't be late again!'

'What did she look like?' asked Flame.

'Who?' asked Marina.

'Verena's grandmother of course, you dope!' said Flame.

'Don't call me a dope! She had blond hair sort of pulled back on her neck – and she stared at me,' said Marina.

'Stared at you?' asked Grandma.

'Yes, she had these really cold eyes and I could feel her watching me as I walked off – like she was boring a hole in my back. It was weird.'

Grandma shivered. 'How strange,' she said, very quietly and looked thoughtful.

As Marina said the words 'really cold eyes', Flame saw

the face in her nightmare. For an instant, she felt the horror of the dream.

To Flame, the summer afternoon suddenly seemed to have become chilly. She shivered – and looked over at Grandma.

Grandma looked at Flame – and noticed her shiver.

I must tell her about my nightmare, thought Flame.

I must tell Flame about my fear, thought Grandma.

Marina noticed the look that passed between Grandma and Flame and thought of the way Verena's grandmother had stared at her – and she shivered too.

For a few seconds, there was silence.

Then Ariel piped up. 'I've got a note from school – can I go and get it?'

'Go on then,' said Mum.

Ariel ran into the house. A minute later, she ran back and handed a crumpled piece of paper to Mum.

'It's from Mr Blenkinsop,' said Mum, unfolding the note. She started to read it. 'He says – he says . . .'

Mum's voice trailed off. She started to laugh.

'What is it?' asked Dad.

Mum looked at the note – and started reading again, trying hard to keep a straight face. 'Mr Blenkinsop says he has to report "an incident" in Ariel's class yesterday, which caused the teacher and class "some distress". He assures the parents and governors that this was a "one-off occurrence" and that it will not happen again. Notice he doesn't tell us what this "incident" was. He says that Mrs Crump is taking a week off to rest and he assures us – how kind of him – that all the health and safety procedures were followed.'

The Sprite family burst out laughing.

'Was this the floating spectacles, Ariel?' asked Mum.

'What's this, Ariel?' asked Dad, laughing. 'What floating spectacles?'

Ariel was startled. She had completely forgotten about Mrs Crump's spectacles – it seemed like weeks ago. She looked round at her sisters.

They looked anxious. So did Grandma.

Then Ariel remembered. She remembered that she must not say anything about magic powers to Mum and Dad.

Just in case Ariel hadn't remembered, Flame dived in and answered for her.

'Mrs Crump's spectacles floated in the air,' said Flame.

'What? How?' asked Dad.

'They lifted off her chest,' said Flame.

'Is this true, Ariel?' asked Dad.

Ariel nodded. 'Yes,' she said. 'Everybody screamed.'

'Mrs Crump fainted,' continued Flame. 'Batty came in and took her off to Nurse and left Monica Fielding in charge, although nobody took any notice of her. There was a terrible din. Then Batty came back and stood there looking cross till it was home time. He said it was a hot afternoon, that everyone was tired and hysterical.'

'Well, spectacles don't usually float in the air!' said Dad. 'I must say it's been a very strange week – what with the sudden appearance and then the sudden disappearance of the slugs, and now floating spectacles. All very strange indeed.'

The Sprite Sisters said nothing.

'Poor Mrs Crump,' mused Mum, sipping her cup of tea. 'She seems such a nice lady.'

'Did you see the spectacles float, Ariel?' asked Dad, picking up a cherry from his plate.

The Sprite Sisters gasped. Oh heck, they thought.

Ariel opened her mouth to answer, then caught Grandma's eye – and remembered.

'I was looking out of the window at the clouds, Daddy,' said Ariel.

Grandma turned away and smiled.

'Do you think spectacles can float in the air?' asked Dad, looking at his youngest daughter.

There was another sharp intake of breath from the older girls.

'Yes, Daddy,' nodded Ariel, with a very serious face.

Flame, Marina and Ash looked aghast. Oh no! What now? they thought.

But Dad laughed. 'Good!' he said. 'There's not enough magic in this world!' He got up and started rolling up his sleeves. 'Right, I'm off to do the garden.'

'Okay girls, time for music practice,' said Mum, standing up. 'You've only three days until the concert.'

And with that, the family left the table. Dad pottered off to the vegetable garden. Mum and Grandma cleared up the tea things and the girls went through to the dining-room and got out their instruments.

'Phew!' said Flame to Ariel. 'It's lucky that Mum and Dad don't seem to take magic seriously.'

Ariel smiled.

Half an hour later, as the Sprite Sisters were doing their practice, and as Mum was waving her hand to conduct them, Ash suddenly shrieked, 'There's Squeak!'

The gerbil was scurrying along the side of the dining room. Ash put down her cello and bow and went in pursuit.

Within a second, music was abandoned. Mum put her hands on her hips and waited.

'I think he's under the sideboard,' said Marina, crouching down on her hands and knees.

'No, he's here now!' said Ash, peering into the fireplace.

'Can you grab him?' asked Flame.

Ash lunged, but the little animal proved a slippery catch and dived under the sideboard.

Ariel started to wail with frustration – and then the phone rang in the hall.

A moment later, Grandma put her head around the door and said, 'It's for you, Ottalie.'

Mum left the dining room – and Grandma came in.

'Use your powers to catch him,' she said, shutting the door.

The Sprite Sisters stopped – and looked at her.

'What – with you here?' said Ash.

'*Yes* – quick!' said Grandma.

As the gerbil ran out from underneath the sideboard, Ariel pointed her finger. Out whooshed her magic power. In a split second, the little animal lifted into the air and Marina caught him, as if catching a rounders ball. She drew Squeak close to her chest and laughed, just as Mum walked back into the room.

'We've got him!' said Ariel.

'Oh, good! I am pleased, love,' said Mum. 'Put him back in his cage. Come on, we must press on with the practice.'

'That was impressive,' Grandma whispered to Ariel.

Ariel giggled.

As the Sprite Sisters resumed their practice, Grandma walked to the kitchen and sat down in the Windsor chair by the Aga. She smiled to herself as she thought about Ariel's magic and for a while she just sat there, thinking about when she was a girl.

It was such fun to have magic powers, she thought. She remembered the way she used to make things fly around her bedroom and pull objects towards her or make them recede. She thought about the way she knew what people were going to say next or who she would meet that day. Then she thought about the birds and animals whose broken bones she had mended, by stroking them lovingly and gently.

That was a lovely feeling, she thought.

As Grandma sat there, deep in her memories, a breeze came through the kitchen like a thin sliver of ice.

Grandma suddenly felt very cold. She shivered and remembered what Marina had said today about feeling watched. She looked around the high-ceilinged kitchen. She was alone, of course – but she had the curious feeling that she was not.

Something is going on, she thought, and she realised that each time she had thought about the school concert today, she had felt worried rather than excited.

Verena's grandmother – who is this woman, really, she thought? Is it her? Is *she* back in my life and out to get me . . . and maybe the girls?

'Are you all right?' asked Mum, as she came into the kitchen and saw Grandma sitting stiffly in the chair. It was unusual to see her like this.

'I'm worried about you: you look pale again,' said Mum.

'It's nothing, love,' said Grandma, trying to smile at her. 'I was just feeling a little tired – must be all this excitement. How did the girls get on?'

'Fine – I think they'll play really well on Friday,' said Mum. 'They all seem very excited, although Flame has looked a bit stressed these last few days. You know what high standards she has.'

'Hmm,' agreed Grandma and she thought about the look that passed between them at tea.

I must talk with her soon, thought Grandma.

CHAPTER ELEVEN

✳

PREMONITIONS

ON THURSDAY mornings, Grandma played bridge with three friends. Each week, they would alternate between their houses.

Today, Maude and Kenneth collected her and drove her to Joan's house, a few miles away. Years ago, Joan and Grandma had been at school together and knew everything – or *almost* everything – about each other. None of Grandma's friends knew of her magic powers, however. It was her one secret.

The four friends sat in the garden and drank coffee, then came inside to play their card game. They were all good bridge players and took it seriously, but they chatted as well.

'Sad news about Verena Glass's mother running off,' said Joan, as she shuffled the pack of cards. 'Poor girl.'

'Yes, bad business,' agreed Kenneth.

'Do you know the grandmother who has come to look after her?' Maude asked Grandma. 'I believe she arrived on Sunday.'

Grandma drew breath. She felt cold suddenly.

'I'm not sure,' she replied.

'Funny that she's turned up to look after Verena now, when she's never shown a shred of interest in the child before,' continued Maude, who always knew the latest gossip. 'She sounds a bit of a cold fish to me – been married four times, apparently. All of her husbands were wealthy, two of them were American millionaires; last one was a lawyer. Seems she's lived abroad most of her life and gone back to her second husband's name. Quite a lady, by the sound of it! Don't know if she's a bridge player.'

'What is her name?' Grandma asked, hesitantly.

'Glenda – Glenda Glass, I believe,' said Maude. 'Oh, yes – and I think she was ballet dancer when she was younger! You may know her, Marilyn.'

Grandma gasped, put her hand to her mouth and dropped her hand of cards on the table.

'Marilyn, are you all right?' Joan stared at her friend, who was now as white as a sheet and holding on to the card table.

'Good heavens!' said Kenneth, jumping up. 'Your teeth are chattering! Come and sit down on the sofa, old girl.'

He helped Grandma out of her chair and led her gently to the sofa. Maude fussed around her with a blanket.

'Here, drink this – it will warm you up,' said Joan, handing Grandma a glass of brandy.

Grandma took a little sip. 'Thank you,' she said. She was shaking all over.

'I think we'd better get you home,' said Kenneth. 'I'll drive you back.'

Grandma agreed. She did not want to play bridge or talk to people, even her dear friends. She wanted to be alone to think and to gather her strength.

Maude and Kenneth saw Grandma safely home to Sprite Towers. Mum opened the front door and insisted she call the doctor. She had never seen her mother-in-law, normally so vibrant and healthy, in this state before.

But Grandma was adamant. 'No doctor, please, dear. I'm fine – *really*. I just need a little lie-down.'

Mum helped Grandma climb the stairs and led her to her bedroom. Grandma lay down on top of the bed and Mum covered her with a blanket. Then Bert came in and lay down beside the bed.

'I'm worried about you,' said Mum.

Grandma closed her eyes. 'I just need a little rest.'

Mum drew the curtains. 'I'll be back shortly,' she said softly.

* * *

An hour later, Grandma opened her eyes and looked around the cream-coloured room, with its huge, flowery curtains, the big soft bed and the rosewood dressing table that Sheldon had bought her when they first married. She loved this room – she felt safe here.

We all feel safe in this house, she thought, safe at Sprite Towers – but the outside world, that's different.

As she lay on the bed, Grandma went through the events that week. She remembered the sudden feeling of threat as she sat in the garden on Sunday afternoon, the cold and shivering she had experienced since then, how she had felt panic on hearing the name Glenda. Then there was the sense of being watched.

It's her – my old enemy, Glenda, thought Grandma. She's back.

Memories flooded through Grandma's mind. She saw herself dancing on the stage, pirouetting and leaping. Oh, how she loved to dance!

I was a wonderful dancer, she thought. I had a real gift.

She thought of Sheldon and how he had smiled at her from his theatre seat, of their first dinner together and how they'd realised they were second cousins. How they'd laughed, how much she had loved him and what a wonderful life they had shared together.

And she felt happy, as she lay on the bed.

Her mood grew heavy, however, as she thought about

how Glenda had nearly ruined her career and tried to spoil her relationship with Sheldon, of the way Glenda had competed with her at every step, of Glenda's jealousy and spite and how she had tried to undermine the *corps de ballet*. She shivered as she remembered their fight in the dark street and how she had hurt Glenda. Since that night, the tingling in her fingers had never come back. She had lost her magic power – but she *had* stopped Glenda. Or had she?

I wonder if Glenda still has her power? she thought.

Somehow she knew she had.

For a few minutes, Grandma lay paralysed with fear, terrified that harm might come to her family. She wondered if Glenda knew – had some sixth sense – that the Sprite Sisters had inherited the Sprite family magic. If so, Grandma felt certain that she would try to expose them, publicly. Exposure would hurt the girls, could weaken their powers.

She'll start with the concert, thought Grandma. That's what she'll do.

I am no good to my granddaughters like this, she thought. I must pull myself together for their sakes.

Mum brought Grandma lunch on a tray and insisted that she rest in her room all afternoon.

Later, Dad came into see her, drew back the curtains and sat down on the bed.

'How are you feeling, Mother?' he asked, taking her hand.

'Much better, love,' she smiled.

'Well don't rush to get up – just take it easy. I'm working at home this afternoon, so just call if you need anything.'

Grandma was sitting in an armchair with Bert on her lap, when she heard her granddaughters arrive home from school. The front door thudded shut and the house exploded with noise and laughter.

What a racket they make, she thought, smiling to herself as she stroked the dog's silky ears.

'Afternoon, Sidney!' the Sprite Sisters shouted at their great-great-grandfather's portrait, as they pelted past, swinging round the huge acorn-shaped newel post at the bottom of the staircase.

Suddenly Grandma's room was full of noisy girls. The Sprite Sisters kissed their grandmother and bent down to stroke Bert. For the next few minutes, the room bubbled with news and laughter.

Flame waited until her younger sisters had left the room then said, 'Grandma, there's something I need to tell you.'

'Sit down, love. There's something *I* need to tell *you*.'

Flame sat on the armchair beside her. Her face was intense and worried.

'What was it you wanted to tell me, Grandma?' she asked.

'I believe that Verena Glass's grandmother is my old enemy, Glenda,' said Grandma.

'*What?* Are you sure?' said Flame, horrified.

'I had this strange, shivery feeling on Sunday afternoon – a feeling of foreboding,' said Grandma. 'It turns out that Verena's grandmother moved in at that time.'

'Ash and I felt something go overhead while we were sitting in the garden,' said Flame. 'It was like a shadow – but there was nothing in the sky!'

'Yes, that's what I felt,' agreed Grandma.

'Then what happened?' asked Flame.

'Several things. First, your father mentioned Verena's grandmother at supper – and I felt icy cold again. When Marina described the woman who drove Verena to school, that got me thinking. Then today, at bridge, my friends were talking about Verena's grandmother – and I found out that her name is Glenda.'

Flame looked at her grandmother, wide-eyed.

'It has to be her,' said Grandma.

For a moment, Flame said nothing. She could feel her heart pounding as she thought about her nightmare.

'The face . . .' she said, biting her lip.

'What face, love?'

'The face in my nightmare,' said Flame.

'What nightmare?'

'That's what I was going to tell you about. I had a nightmare on Monday night,' said Flame, speaking quickly. Her cheeks were flushed and her eyes wide. 'We were all up on stage at the concert, but when we started playing everything went wrong. We made the most awful noise and were out of time. I stood up to apologise to the audience – and saw the face of a woman. She was about your age and she had a sharp nose and cold eyes. She was laughing at us and I knew, somehow, that *she'd* made it all go wrong. I didn't know what to do. It was horrible.'

'Oh sweetie, you should have told me – I noticed you looked pale,' said Grandma, and she hugged her granddaughter tight.

For a moment they were silent.

Then Grandma said, 'Listen, Flame. I think Glenda might try to sabotage your performance at the concert. It's a feeling I have – and it would explain your nightmare. It sounds as if we have both had a premonition.'

'What do you think she'll do?' asked Flame. She felt sick.

'We don't know if Glenda still has her magic power, but I think we must assume she has, otherwise we would not have had these warnings,' said Grandma. 'I'm telling you this because you're older than the other girls. We don't want to frighten them, but they do need to know – and you have to work out a plan.'

'A plan?' asked Flame.

'Yes, a plan to stop her,' said Grandma.

'But we don't know what she will do.'

Grandma stared at the carpet for a few moments.

'You're right – we don't. If only I still had my powers I could show you how to defend yourselves, as my grandmother taught me. But you girls need to work it out for yourselves.' Grandma looked up suddenly and smiled at Flame. 'Don't worry, I know you'll think of something.'

Everyone was pleased to see Grandma looking brighter when she came down for supper.

Afterwards, the Sprite Sisters practised their music. Mum noticed Flame seemed a little distracted and her sisters seemed aware of it too. Despite this, they all played beautifully.

'Wonderful!' said Mum, when they finished.

As they packed up their instruments, Marina asked Flame, 'What were you and Grandma talking about? You seem anxious about something. What's happened?'

Flame took a deep breath.

'There's something I need to tell you all about,' she said. 'We'll have to talk once we've gone up to bed.'

'Okay,' said Marina, looking worried. 'I hope it's nothing nasty.'

On the way up to bed, Ariel stopped to talk to Sidney Sprite's portrait. She was standing in front of the picture hanging on the wall at the bottom of the mahogany staircase when Marina came through the hallway.

'What are you doing?' asked Marina, poking her in the ribs. 'I heard you! Were you talking to Sidney?'

'I was telling him we'd found the gerbils,' replied Ariel. 'He's very pleased.'

'Don't be ridiculous! How can he be pleased? He's dead!' Marina burst out laughing.

Ariel looked at her sister with a perfectly straight face. 'Sidney sees everything that is going on in this house,' she said.

'That's silly!' said Marina. 'Come on, race you to the top! Night, Sidney!'

The two girls turned and bounded up the stairs.

'I do wish you would stop running up the stairs like that!' shouted Mum, who was waiting for them at the top. 'You'll wear out the carpet. Come on, it's bathtime.'

When Mum had gone downstairs after their baths and all was quiet, Flame, Ash and Ariel went into Marina's bedroom and sat on her bed. It was almost dark and there was a faint chill in the air.

Marina's room was painted yellow and there were books and clothes everywhere. Marina liked it that way. She called it a 'glorious muddle'.

The Sprite Sisters sat in their pyjamas on the stripy blue and white duvet.

'Ariel was talking to Sidney,' teased Marina. 'Silly!'

Flame and Ash laughed.

'You are a funny little thing!' said Flame.

'Well, I sometimes get the feeling Sidney sees everything, too,' admitted Ash.

'If Sidney had magic powers, Sprite Towers itself might

be magic,' said Ariel, wide-eyed.

Her three older sisters looked at Ariel, amazed by the clarity of this insight.

Flame looked thoughtful. 'There's an idea . . .' she murmured.

'I'll bet the towers are magic,' said Ash.

'Cool!' said Marina.

'I love Sprite Towers,' said Ash. 'I hope we can always live here together.'

'What, even when we're old ladies?' said Ariel.

'Especially when we're old ladies,' said Ash. 'But we'll lock you in the cellar if you get too noisy!'

'Do you think there are ghosts here?' asked Marina.

'*I've* never seen one,' said Ash.

'Perhaps we haven't looked hard enough,' said Marina. 'Are you all right, Flame? You seem awfully quiet. What was that thing you wanted to tell us about?'

The three sisters looked at Flame. She stared down at the duvet, as if gathering her thoughts.

'What's happened?' asked Ash, worried.

Flame sat up straight, looked at her sisters and said, 'Grandma is pretty sure that Verena's grandmother is her old enemy, Glenda.'

'*What?*' said Marina.

'And I think she was the face in my nightmare,' added Flame.

'Oh heck!' said Ash.

'Will she hurt us?' asked Ariel.

'Grandma thinks Glenda probably still has her magic powers,' said Flame. 'And she thinks Glenda may want to expose our powers.'

'Blimey,' said Marina.

As the dark gathered around them, the Sprite Sisters huddled closer together on the bed.

'Why would Verena's grandmother want to hurt us?' said Ariel. 'I don't understand.'

'She wants to hurt Grandma,' said Flame. 'They were bitter dancing rivals and Glenda must still hate Grandma. If she hurts *us*, that will hurt Grandma more than anything. Glenda has dark magic powers – Grandma said so – and she won't want us to have any magic powers. She knows if she exposes us our powers could weaken.'

The Sprite Sisters were silent as they thought about this. Marina pulled at her hair, her eyes glazed. Ash clasped her hands together and looked at them. Flame stared into space and chewed the skin round her thumbnail.

Then Ariel said in a small voice, 'I'm frightened. I've never played in a big concert before – and this one is really important for the school. I only got my magic powers on Sunday. Now I might lose them forever. It's too much to think about all at once, when you're nine.'

For a moment it felt to the Sprite Sisters as if they might all burst into tears.

Marina broke the mood. 'Come on, sugar plum,' she

said, hugging Ariel. 'We'll all stick together and I bet we'll find a way to outwit that nasty old witch, Glenda Glass!'

Ariel giggled, hugging Marina back.

Flame and Ash looked thoughtful.

'We need a plan,' said Flame. Ash nodded.

The Sprite Sisters were quiet for a moment.

'Let's make the Circle of Power again,' said Ariel. 'That'll cheer you up, Flame.'

'Good idea,' said Flame, and the other girls nodded. They shuffled round the bed and formed a circle.

'Is that right?' asked Marina.

'Yes, that's it,' said Flame. 'Our powers are balanced. East, south, west and north. It's as if we have a protective shield around us.'

They held hands.

'I am Fire,' said Flame.

'I am Water,' said Marina.

'I am Earth,' said Ash.

'And I'm – I'm . . . what am I?' asked Ariel.

'Air,' said Flame. 'Like your name.'

'Yes, I'm Air,' said Ariel, with a dreamy smile. 'I like being Air.'

As Ariel spoke, the bright blue light started to glow around them, as if moving through their arms from body to body. The light got stronger and stronger.

'It feels all fizzy!' laughed Ariel.

'Hold together!' said Flame. 'Don't break the circle.'

'It's amazing – it feels like nothing could hurt us when we do this,' said Ash. 'It really feels like a Circle of Power.'

The girls were laughing and the bright blue light was shining as the bedroom door opened and Mum turned on the light.

Instantly, the sisters dropped their hands – and the blue light went out.

'*Whatever* are you all doing?' said Mum. 'It's ten o'clock and you should have been asleep ages ago. You've got a big day ahead of you tomorrow.'

'Sorry, Mum,' everyone said. Flame, Ash and Ariel clambered off Marina's bed.

'Now, back to your rooms and straight to sleep,' said Mum. 'You are all getting too excited about the concert.'

'Do you think Mum saw the light?' Ash whispered to Flame, as they walked up the corridor to their bedrooms.

Flame shook her head. 'It's funny, but I don't think she did. I wonder if it's only us who can see it?'

'What would she say if she found out?' asked Ash.

'I don't know,' said Flame. She turned to Ariel. 'Ariel, please don't say anything to Mum.'

'Don't worry, Flame, I won't,' said Ariel, closing her bedroom door.

'Mum, have you ever seen any ghosts in this house?' asked Marina, as Mum tucked her in again.

'No, love. Why do you ask?'

'Oh, just wondered. Night, Mum.'

Mum turned out the light, checked on the other three sisters, then walked back down the wide mahogany staircase.

Meanwhile, as the Sprite Sisters settled in their beds at Sprite Towers, a mile away at The Oaks, Verena Glass said goodnight to her grandmother. There were no hugs or kisses.

For the past two hours, Verena and Glenda Glass had watched television, sitting at opposite ends of the sofa. Only a few words had passed between them and neither said anything to the other about the Sprite family, though both were thinking of them.

'Goodnight,' said Glenda, with a brief nod.

'Goodnight,' said Verena, and closed the living-room door.

Grandma hardly notices me, she thought, as she climbed the stairs to her bedroom. *I wonder what it would be like to have a family that laughed together and hugged each other, like the Sprites? I wonder if the sisters race each other upstairs when they go to bed?*

Verena turned on the lamp, drew the curtains and looked around her large, sumptuously decorated bedroom.

This evening, though, it just felt empty.

Downstairs, Glenda Glass sat in the gathering dark, her sharp profile lit up only by the glow of the television screen.

Not long now, she thought. *Not long, little Sprites.*

CHAPTER TWELVE

✳

THE PLAN AND OSWALD'S OFFER

✳ ✳

✳

THERE WAS an air of mounting excitement at Drysdale's School on Friday morning. The pupils playing or singing in the inter-schools concert had their final rehearsal and it went well. The instruments were ready; the stage was set. By lunchtime, everyone was optimistic that Drysdale's would win the regional competition.

Flame was hanging up her school blazer in the cloakroom, when Verena Glass walked past.

Verena stopped and, as if she had just remembered it, said to Flame, 'Quinn is coming to the concert this evening. He knows I am to be star of the show. He told me he was really looking forward to hearing me sing – but then everybody is.' Verena smiled a withering smile as she delivered this piece of news.

Flame's cheeks flushed with anger and it took all her self-control to stay silent. Quinn had not told her he was looking forward to hearing *her* play – but then she hadn't seen him in the last two days. It was also nonsense for Verena to claim she was the star act – but that was Verena.

Flame turned around and looked into Verena's cold blue eyes: they were level with her own.

I wonder if Verena knows we are distant cousins? she thought.

'You are *one* of the star acts, Verena,' said Flame, quietly, but firmly. 'Quinn is coming to the concert to see his sister play.'

Verena was taken aback by the intensity of Flame's gaze and took half a step back. She was annoyed. It used to be so easy to make Flame Sprite angry, she thought.

Flame picked up her bag and started to walk away. She hated the idea that Quinn liked Verena more than her.

'I hope those little sisters of yours manage to stay in time this evening,' Verena sniped at Flame's back. 'We have a lot of competition from the other schools and it would be a shame if they let Drysdale's down.'

Her words hit Flame's back like an arrow. For a split second, Flame hesitated. She was tempted to spit back that at least she *had* sisters and that Verena was a spoiled only child.

She turned round to face Verena and took a step forward. 'Why would my sisters let down the school?' said Flame.

Verena's lip curled in a sneer. 'You Sprite Sisters go about like there's something magical about you all and as if nothing could hurt you.'

Flame gasped.

Did Verena know about their magic? Had her grandmother told her about the Sprite Sisters' powers?

For the second time that week, Flame remembered the 'ping' moment – and she knew she should not rise to Verena's taunts.

'We want to win the inter-schools competition as much as everybody else,' she said. 'There's no way we'd let Drysdale's down.'

She turned and walked away.

I wonder if Verena knows about her grandmother's magic power, she thought?

Some part of her told her that Verena was unaware.

Flame kept on walking.

Marina, Ash and Ariel were in high spirits when Dad collected them from school that afternoon. The concert was now only three hours away.

Flame sat in the back of the car and looked out of the

window. She was wondering how to stop Glenda Glass spoiling their performance.

'We need to work out our plan for Glenda,' she whispered to Marina as they got out of the car.

'Mmm, I know,' replied Marina absent-mindedly.

Flame sighed.

The Sprite Sisters ate chocolate cake and drank glasses of homemade lemonade on the terrace, then they all ran down the garden. Ariel, Ash and Marina began a raucous game of tag on the lawn. Flame sat on the swing under the big lime tree, dragging her shoes on the grass.

How can I stop this woman hurting us? she thought. There is so little time! What shall I do? If my sisters understand the danger, why aren't they helping me to work out what to do?

I have to solve this myself, thought Flame.

She leaned back on the swing and looked up to the leaf canopy. She watched the afternoon sunlight flicker through the millions of leaves above her and her mind relaxed in the shimmering green.

Suddenly, she had an idea. She remembered how powerful she and her sisters had felt when they sat holding hands and formed the Circle of Power.

That's it, she thought – *that's* what we must do.

Flame jumped off the swing and ran back to the house. Grandma had just arrived home from grocery shopping and was standing alone in the kitchen.

'Grandma, I think I know how to stop Glenda hurting us!' she said.

'Thank heavens!' said Grandma, putting down a bag on the table.

'The other morning – you know, Sunday, when Ariel found her power?' said Flame.

'Yes?'

'Well, we were all sitting on my bed and talking about it. I suggested we hold hands – so we did, and it was amazing! And since then we've done it twice, and the same thing happens!'

'What happens?' asked Grandma.

'Well, this bright blue light whizzes around us – through our bodies,' said Flame. 'I call it the Circle of Power, because that's what it feels like. It feels like nothing can hurt us.'

'Yes, that's what it is,' said Grandma. 'You're right. That is your defence. Glenda will not be able to hurt you if you are balanced together. Thank goodness you have found your protection in time. Remember, nothing happens by chance in life.'

'But what should we do?' asked Flame. 'We can't hold hands and play our instruments at the same time.'

'No, but you could sit in a circle and focus your thoughts together,' said Grandma.

'But how will I explain it to Mr Taylor, the music

master?' asked Flame. 'One of us will have to sit with our back to the audience. It will look so odd! We always sit in a half-circle, facing out towards the audience.'

'It doesn't matter,' said Grandma. 'Go and tell your sisters – quickly, we have to leave soon. Explain it to them simply and calmly. Assure them that if you do this, all will be okay, but don't say anything to your mother or your teachers or anyone else. When you get on to the stage, move the chairs into a circle. Do it confidently and everybody will think that's what you always do.'

Flame ran down to the bottom of the garden. Her sisters were feeding the rabbits and guinea pigs.

'I have a plan for thwarting Glenda Glass!' she said, as she came up to them.

'What?' They all looked at Flame.

'We have to sit in a circle on stage and make the Circle of Power!' Flame burst out.

'What will that do?' asked Ash, stuffing grass into a hutch.

'Protect us from Glenda's magic power,' said Flame.

'But couldn't one of us use our magic powers to stop her when we come on to the stage?' asked Marina.

'We are not powerful enough to stop her on our own,' said Flame.

'How do you know?' asked Ash.

'We are too young: Grandma says that magic powers usually get stronger as you get older,' said Flame. 'Besides,

Grandma has always told us we must not use our magic to hurt anyone. I can't just walk out on stage, point a finger at Glenda and burn her to smithereens.'

Marina, Ash and Ariel looked at their elder sister. They trusted her.

'The danger we face is our magic powers being publicly exposed – and that exposure would mean we'd lose them,' said Flame, quietly. 'That would be tragic.'

The sisters were silent for a moment.

'I don't want the horrid lady to hurt us,' said Ariel. 'I'm frightened.'

'No, don't be frightened!' her older sisters said together.

'There's four of us and one of her!' said Marina.

'And I have never played on stage before,' said Ariel.

'You'll be fine, pumpkin,' said Flame, stroking Ariel's hair. 'We'll all be together.'

'So how do we do it?' asked Ash.

'We have to put our seats in a circle,' said Flame.

'Then what happens?' asked Marina.

'We've got to play our instruments – but we've also got to focus on forming the Circle of Power,' explained Flame.

'It sounds awfully complicated,' said Marina.

Flame gave Marina a look. 'I agree – but I don't think we have any choice. It's that or public exposure of our magic powers by retaliating against Glenda – *and* letting down Drysdale's.'

Marina swallowed hard. 'Yes, I see what you mean –

but it is going to look really odd. One of us is going to have their back to the audience. We have never played like that before on stage. Is this really the only way we can do it?'

'Well, what ideas have *you* got for dealing with Glenda?' asked Flame, sharply.

Marina shrugged. 'I haven't,' she replied.

'It feels like I'm doing all the thinking here – as usual,' said Flame.

'That's not fair, Flame!' said Marina, moving forward and throwing up her hands. 'You always do this!'

'What?' asked Flame, facing her younger sister.

'Think you have to solve everything on your own,' said Marina.

'We are in danger here – but you don't seem to be worried!' said Flame. 'I'm open to other ideas, but we'll be on stage in a couple of hours! For heaven's sake, if you have an idea, then say so now!'

Tears of frustration poured down Flame's cheeks.

'Hey, sis,' said Ash, stepping forwards and putting an arm around her older sister. 'Calm down. We're all in this together. I think your idea is a good one, Flame – and as you say, it's the only one we've got. I think we should make the Circle of Power. It's our strongest defence.'

'Thank you,' said Flame, relaxing a bit.

Marina looked thoughtful. 'You're right, Flame,' she said, taking a step back. 'But remember – it's not *you* against Glenda: it's *us* against Glenda.'

At that moment, the big brass bell by the kitchen door rang.

'Suppertime,' said Flame. 'We have to go in.' She paused. Then she said, 'Do you all understand what we have to do?'

Marina, Ash and Ariel nodded.

'Right, let's go then,' said Flame.

'Race you back!' said Ariel. Marina and Ash bolted off and they all dashed over the lawn.

Flame walked back alone, deep in thought.

As they washed their hands, Marina asked Flame, 'Do you really think we'll be okay this evening?'

'Yes,' replied Flame, every inch the eldest sister. 'We'll be fine.'

Inside though, Flame was nervous. Glenda's face, so full of menace, came into her mind – and she shuddered.

The family sat down for an early supper and the big Sprite Towers kitchen hummed with voices. There was an atmosphere of excitement.

Mum and Grandma lifted plates and food out of the Aga.

Amongst the hubbub, Flame approached Grandma and said quietly, 'I've told them.'

'Well done, love,' said Grandma.

Flame turned back towards the table.

'Flame,' came her grandmother's voice behind her, quick but insistent.

'Yes?'

'Resolve.'

Flame saw the strength in her grandmother's eyes and nodded. She understood.

They were about halfway through supper when the phone rang. Dad got up to answer it. The family stopped talking.

'Hello, Colin Sprite,' said Dad.

'Hello, Colin, old chap – Oswald Foffington-Plinker here,' said the voice at the other end of the telephone.

Dad made a face at his family as if to say 'Urgh!' and walked out of the kitchen to the hallway, the phone at his ear.

'Hello, Oswald,' he answered. 'What can I do for you?'

Dad could not abide Oswald Foffington-Plinker: he said the man made his flesh creep. Foffington-Plinker was a successful property developer and was known as a ruthless businessman.

As an architect, however, Dad did not want to upset any local property developers, however much he disliked them. He had never worked with Foffington-Plinker, and had no intention of doing so, but theirs was a town where everyone knew everyone.

And there were other connections: Foffington-Plinker was Verena Glass's uncle – his sister was her errant mother and Verena's father was a distant Sprite cousin.

Most of all, there was the roof – Dad's biggest challenge. If his family were to remain at Sprite Towers and keep his daughters at Drysdale's School, then he needed to earn a lot more money.

Dad drew a deep breath, but nothing could have prepared him for what Oswald was about to suggest.

'I understand you're going to be at the school concert this evening,' said Oswald.

'Yes, the girls are all playing,' said Dad, warily.

'Good, good,' said Oswald. 'It should be a lovely evening. I shall be going, of course. My niece, Verena is singing, you know.'

'Yes,' replied Dad. He wondered what this conversation was really about.

'Actually, I wondered if we could have a chat,' said Oswald, in his oily voice. 'The thing is, old chap, I'd like to buy your house.'

'*What?*' said Dad. 'But it's not for sale!'

'I'm aware you haven't put it on the market,' said Oswald. 'But I'll make you a very generous offer. Think of all the upkeep you'd save, keeping that big old rambling place in one piece. Maintaining the roof alone must be costing you a fortune. Think about it, old chap. I'd make you a rich man.'

'I do not want to be a rich man, Oswald – I'm perfectly happy as I am,' said Dad. 'But why on earth would you want to buy Sprite Towers?'

'I think it would convert perfectly to a boutique hotel – twenty luxury bedrooms, designer interiors, spa – you know the sort of thing,' replied Oswald. 'And I'd like to develop the site – you've got a big garden, so there's lots of space to build on, loads of potential. I know business has been tricky for you lately, old chap . . . Well, I'd be able to offer you plenty of work – lots of new buildings for you to design. And you could have a lovely executive home in the grounds – or maybe we could develop the stable block for your family? I thought we could have a word about it this evening – or I could pop round tomorrow and have a look round . . .'

In the kitchen, Mum, Grandma and the sisters ate silently. They could hear Dad's voice in the hallway and sensed something was amiss. He sounded very tense.

Mum got up, opened the kitchen door and looked at her husband. Dad was standing with his mouth open and one hand clutching his forehead.

'Oswald, *Sprite Towers is not for sale!*' said Dad. 'I'm sorry, but that's an end to the matter. Now I must go and finish eating my supper. Goodbye.'

Dad clicked off the phone.

Mum held the door open for him as he walked past into the kitchen, his face white with rage.

It was not often that Colin Sprite got angry, but when did, he got volcanic.

'Oswald Foffington-Plinker?' guessed Mum.

'Yes,' replied Dad, very, very quietly. His knuckles were

white as his hands gripped the table.

The Sprite Sisters stared. They had never seen their father look so upset.

'What is it, Daddy?' asked Ariel, her eyes like saucers.

Grandma and Mum exchanged anxious glances.

'Colin? What did he want, love?' asked Mum.

They waited.

'He's mad!' exploded Dad, banging his hand on the table. Everybody jumped. 'Says he wants to buy Sprite Towers and turn it into a *boutique hotel*! A boutique hotel, for heaven's sake! Have you ever heard anything so ridiculous?'

The Sprite Sisters' mouths dropped open.

'No, he can't do that – *we* live here!' said Marina, tears welling up in her eyes.

Mum took her hand and squeezed it. 'It's all right, sweetie, nobody is going to take Sprite Towers away from us,' she said.

Dad looked at Mum. 'He threatened me, Ottalie! He said he could make a great deal of difference to my professional life. I know what he meant – he seemed to know I needed more work, and he can put on the screws. Kept calling me "old chap". Urgh, loathsome man!'

Mum looked at Dad. 'It'll be fine,' she said, calmly.

He nodded, gritting his teeth, then got up and walked to the kitchen door. 'Sorry, love – I've had enough to eat,' he said.

Mum smiled at him. 'That's fine.'

'Think I'll go down the garden for a little while.' And he opened the back door and stomped off over the lawn.

'Right, girls, let's get ready,' said Mum, gathering up the plates. 'We need to leave in twenty minutes. Go and wash your hands and brush your hair.'

Ash did not go to wash her hands or tidy her hair. Instead, she ran down the garden. Dad was standing near the potting shed, looking at his vegetable garden. Ash came and stood beside him and took his hand in hers. He smiled down at her. He looked a little sad. Ash smiled up at him.

'The spinach is doing really well,' she said.

'Yes, it is,' he nodded and squeezed her hand tight.

Fifteen minutes later, the Sprite family climbed into two cars. Mum drove the four girls in her big old car. Dad drove Grandma in his old, racing green-coloured sports car: its *broom, broom* noise always cheered him up.

And off they went to the school concert.

Mum noticed her daughters were very quiet.

Flame, Marina, Ash and Ariel stared out of the car windows. They were thinking of what lay ahead: their first public musical performance and their first battle using their magic powers.

'You all okay?' asked Mum.

'Yes, Mum,' they answered.

'No need to be nervous – just enjoy it,' said Mum. 'It's going to be a wonderful evening.'

'It will certainly be a memorable one,' said Flame – and her sisters smiled.

In the racing green-coloured sports car, Dad wrestled with the gears, swung round corners and started to relax.

Grandma, on the other hand, was feeling tense.

'You look worried, Mother,' said Dad. 'What's up? Is it my driving?'

'Just thinking about the girls, dear – I hope they're okay,' she replied.

'They'll be fine – they've rehearsed enough!' laughed Dad.

'Yes, you're right,' smiled Grandma.

If only you knew, she thought. If only you knew what happened all those years ago – and what Glenda Glass is capable of. And in a matter of minutes, I shall meet her again.

CHAPTER THIRTEEN

THE SCHOOL CONCERT

BATTY BLENKINSOP, the headmaster, gave the Sprite family a warm welcome as they walked into the school hall on Friday at six-thirty p.m. The Sprites contributed a lot to Drysdale's: the four Sprite Sisters were keen participants in sport and music; Dad was a school governor, Mum taught piano and singing to pupils in the senior school and both parents gave unstinting support at events and matches. In addition, Batty and Dad were cricketing friends who played together at the local village cricket club and for the Old Drysdalians' team.

A tall, diffident man in his early fifties, Batty

Blenkinsop was a much-liked, if somewhat uncharismatic, headmaster. His misfortune was to be married to a woman called Virginia who the Sprite Sisters had nicknamed 'the Gargoyle'. This frog-faced woman had the loudest voice ever heard. Not surprisingly most of the pupils tended to give her a wide berth.

That evening, the Gargoyle was standing beside her husband and greeted the Sprites as warmly as she could, which was not very.

'Hello girls!' she boomed. 'I hope you'll do Drysdale's proud this evening!'

The Sprite Sisters smiled politely.

'Get yourselves a good seat!' said Batty, shaking Mum, Dad and Grandma's hands. Then he turned away to greet the next set of parents.

The Sprite family looked smart that evening, as they walked through the grand hall. Dad cut a dash in a linen suit and tie, Mum wore a flowery summer dress and had piled up her curly hair, while Grandma looked elegant in a red linen sheath dress. The Sprite Sisters wore their school uniform and had all brushed their hair.

The walls of the school hall were covered in dark wood panels with framed lists of headteachers and head pupils that went back years and years. The hall had a high ceiling and a dark oak floor and it smelled of floor polish. When Old Drysdalians visited the school, even decades later, it was the familiar smell of floor polish in the hall that evoked the memory of their school days.

'Where would you like to sit?' Dad asked Mum and Grandma, as they walked up the centre aisle. Around them were five hundred chairs laid out in rows for the concert.

'Near the front on the left, I think, love,' said Mum.

Dad stopped at the second row from the front. 'Here okay? The front row is saved for the judges.'

'Yes, fine,' agreed Mum. 'This good for you, Mother?'

Grandma would have preferred to sit further back, where she could see Glenda, but she said nothing.

How could I explain? she thought. Besides, I haven't any idea where Glenda will sit.

'Yes, that's fine, dear,' she agreed.

'Girls, I assume you'll be sitting backstage for the first half, when you're not playing?' Dad asked them.

'Yes,' nodded Flame, casting an eye around the hall to see if Glenda had arrived. She noticed that Grandma was looking a little pale.

Dad placed their programmes on the seats, but it was still quite early, so they stayed standing up. The Sprites were a popular family; many of their friends would be here this evening and this would be a chance to catch up with them.

'Hello there!' people kept saying to them and they'd all start chatting.

Ash and Ariel went backstage to help Mr Taylor set up. Flame and Marina did not want to leave Grandma alone to face Glenda, however, so they waited with her and their parents. Any minute now, Glenda and Verena would arrive.

'I feel sick,' Marina whispered to Flame.

'You're getting too tense – just relax,' replied Flame, though her own stomach was in tight knots.

'It's not surprising!' retorted Marina.

Flame took her arm. 'We'll be fine. Let's plan how we're going to sit.'

The two sisters walked to the front of the school hall and looked up at the stage. Mum, Dad and Grandma were ten metres away.

'Which way is north?' said Flame, looking round the hall.

'Well, at lunchtime the sun is over that way – so that must be south,' said Marina, pointing towards the windows that ran the length of one side of the school hall.

'That makes sense,' said Flame. 'Okay, if that direction is south, that means east is over there,' said Flame, pointing to the back of the stage. 'I'm east, so if I sit there, I can look out and see Glenda. That's good.'

'It means Ash will sit at the front of the stage, with her back to the audience – that's west,' said Marina.

'I think she'll be okay with that,' said Flame.

'It's going to look so odd!' said Marina.

'We don't have a choice,' murmured Flame.

'Right, well, my power is the south, so that means I'll be on your left – over there,' said Marina, resolutely. She pointed to the right-hand side of the stage from where the audience would be looking. Then Ariel, who is the north, will be on your right hand,' said Marina, pointing to the left-hand side of the stage.

No sooner had Flame and Marina agreed their seating plan than Flame noticed Verena and her family entering the concert hall. They were talking to Batty and the Gargoyle.

Flame touched Marina's arm. 'Glenda is here.'

The two sisters immediately walked towards their family and stood either side of Grandma.

Grandma drew a sharp breath: she knew what this meant. She did not turn, however, though her heart had started to beat very quickly. Instead, she pulled herself up tall, stood as straight as a dancer – and kept her back towards the Glass family who were now approaching up the centre aisle towards the Sprites.

When Flame turned and saw Glenda Glass's face, she gasped: it was the face in her nightmare.

'It *is* her!' she whispered.

'Resolve,' Grandma reminded her.

Flame breathed out slowly and tried to stay calm.

Verena Glass and a tall, elegant woman dressed in a beautifully-cut lilac silk dress and jacket led the party. Behind them were Verena's uncle, Oswald Foffington-Plinker and his wife, Gloria; he wore dark glasses and she teetered on high heels and clutched a huge gold handbag.

As the Glass family approached, Grandma turned to face them.

Dad and Mum stopped talking to their friends and moved forwards.

Glenda Glass and Marilyn Sprite, distant cousins, once rival ballerinas and rivals in love, faced each other in the school hall and stood a metre or so apart. They were a similar height and build and anyone seeing them together might have realised they were related. In many ways, the two women looked remarkably alike, with their sharp features and sophisticated dress sense; but, where one looked warm, the other looked icy cold.

Glenda's blue eyes were fixed and unblinking – like a snake's – on her rival.

'My, my. Marilyn Sprite – we meet again,' said Glenda, her mouth twisting into a sneer.

'Hello, Glenda,' said Grandma.

Neither woman moved forward to kiss or even shake hands.

'It has been a long time,' said Glenda.

'Indeed,' said Grandma. 'You look well.'

'So do you.'

Glenda Glass looked at the two Sprite Sisters standing beside their grandmother.

She looks as if she is sizing us up for lunch, thought Marina.

'Quite a bodyguard you have here,' said Glenda to

Grandma. 'How sweet – these must be your granddaughters. I have heard so much about them. I am so looking forward to hearing them play.'

Flame felt woozy, as if she was back in her bed, covered in sweat, staring at the face in her nightmare.

Mum and Dad exchanged surprised glances.

'I'm Colin Sprite,' said Dad, moving forwards with his right hand out. 'You must be Verena's grandmother, Glenda Glass. I didn't realise you and my mother knew each other.'

Glenda turned and looked Dad up and down. He was taken aback by her gaze, but smiled politely and kept his hand out. Glenda held out her hand, but as Dad tried to shake it, she pulled it back. Dad was left holding the ends of her fingers.

He always told his daughters you could tell a lot about someone by their handshake. Here, he had the sensation of someone cold and calculating. Her handshake, her cold eyes, and her rudeness to his family, particularly to his mother – everything about Glenda Glass made him immediately wary.

It was Oswald Foffington-Plinker who broke the icy chill around the group.

'Hello, old chap!' he smarmed, moving forward and pumping Dad's hand, as if they were old mates.

A second later, he had his arm round Dad's shoulder and was talking into his ear. Dad tried to shake him off, but Oswald stuck to him like a limpet.

Verena was standing beside her grandmother.

'Hello, Verena! How are you?' said Mum, smiling.

'Hello, Mrs Sprite – I'm very well, thank you,' replied Verena. She may not have liked Flame and her sisters, but she had always liked Ottalie Sprite: she was the one mother of her fellow pupils who did not seem to be wary of her.

'Good luck this evening, dear,' said Mum.

'Thank you, Mrs Sprite,' Verena smiled.

The exchange was not lost on Glenda, who cast a cold eye over Mum.

Meanwhile, backstage, Mr Taylor, the music master, had asked Ash and Ariel Sprite to put out the sheet music for the junior orchestra, which was to open the concert. Ash was at one side of the open stage, Ariel at the other, and they were working their way towards the centre, carefully placing several pages of music on each of the stands.

The school hall was rapidly filling up with people. Standing in the centre aisle, Glenda looked up at the stage and noticed the two younger Sprite Sisters.

Hmm, she thought. Time for a little fun with my magic powers.

She lifted her fingers, as if about to touch her face – and as she did so, a huge, invisible beam of energy flew out of her hand.

Immediately, at opposite ends of the stage, Ash and Ariel seemed to trip. It was as if they had both stumbled over a big, invisible log at the same moment.

And, as the two sisters fell to the floor, their sheet piles of music lifted high into the air. Dozens of pieces of paper floated and twirled in the air as if a big wind had whooshed underneath them and held them, suspended.

Then, all at once, the sheets of music rained down all over the stage. The whole stage was covered in white paper. Ash and Ariel picked themselves up from the stage floor and looked in horror at the sea of paper. The audience, still settling in their seats, were laughing a little nervously.

'What happened?' Ariel asked Ash.

'I tripped – but there was nothing in front of me,' whispered Ariel.

'Me, too,' said Ariel. Ash noticed she looked shaken.

Down on the hall floor, Mum had seen her daughters fall.

'Oh my goodness!' she exclaimed. 'Flame, Marina – quick! Go and help your sisters!'

Mum looked round at Glenda Glass and noticed that she was smiling.

What a cruel face she has, thought Mum.

Glenda smiled at Grandma – a killer smile.

As soon as the girls fell, Grandma knew that Glenda had caused the accident – and Glenda knew that she knew it.

'I expect they're warming up for tonight's performance,' said Glenda.

Then she turned abruptly and said, 'Oswald, let's sit down.'

Glenda Glass and Oswald and Gloria Foffington-Plinker moved to their seats in the fourth row.

'Better take our seats,' said Dad to Mum and Grandma and they moved to the second row, just behind the judges.

By the time Flame and Marina got to their sisters on the stage, Ariel was trying hard not to cry.

'I don't know why I fell over,' she said to her elder sisters. 'It was as if something pulled my legs out from under me.'

Flame, Marina and Ash looked at one another.

Ash nodded. 'That's what I felt too,' she said.

'It's Glenda – she used her magic power to trip you up,' said Flame.

'Oh heck,' said Marina. 'We haven't even started playing yet.'

'Maybe she's had her fun,' said Ash. 'Ariel, she may leave us alone now.'

'Do you think so?' Ariel's face brightened.

Ash did not think so, nor did Flame and Marina, but they did not want their little sister to go to pieces before the concert had even begun.

'Everything all right, girls?' asked Mr Taylor, walking out on to the stage.

'Yes, sir, we're fine,' said Flame. 'We'll soon have the music sorted.'

Several pupils came out on to the stage to help collect

and sort the music. In a short while, everything was ready and the stage was set.

The four Sprite Sisters were all members of the junior orchestra. They ran to get their instruments from back-stage.

Down in the audience, Mum whispered to Dad, 'What was that all about with Glenda Glass and your mother, Colin? They were very hostile to one another: did you notice? I had no idea your mother knew her. She's never spoken of her.'

Dad shrugged his shoulders. 'Nor had I. Search me what it was about – but I did notice.'

'Glenda looked so *angry*,' whispered Mum.

'Yes, it was very strange indeed,' agreed Dad.

Sitting the other side of Dad, Grandma heard none of this: she was deep in thought. She sat still and tall in her seat.

I wish I had eyes in the back of my head and could see what Glenda is up to, she thought.

She was furious that Glenda had – even before the concert had begun – deliberately caused Ash and Ariel to fall and drop their music sheets.

Who knows what Glenda will try to do? thought Grandma. I know what she is capable of.

It was hard to believe that Glenda was still jealous and angry after all these years. Grandma breathed a heavy sigh. I hope the girls will be all right, she thought.

Glenda Glass sat on the end of the centre aisle two

rows behind Grandma. From here, she had a perfect and unhindered view of the stage.

The junior orchestra took up their places. The audience settled in their seats and applauded warmly as Batty Blenkinsop walked out to the front of the stage, up to the microphone.

'It is with great pleasure that Drysdale's School is competing this evening in the National Schools Music Competition,' he said into the microphone. 'Many months of hard work and practice have gone into tonight's performances and I can promise you a wonderful evening's entertainment: we have some fine musicians here tonight.'

Everyone applauded.

Batty continued. 'As you all know, tonight's performance is the last of eight concerts given by schools in this region with the judges in attendance. After this concert, the judges will pick the best school in the region, and the chosen school will perform at the national final in London in two weeks' time. It is a tremendous opportunity for Drysdale's and we wish our musicians and teachers the very best of luck.'

There was more applause as Batty left the stage and took his seat in the front row, beside the Gargoyle and the judges.

The junior school orchestra got off to a roaring start. The

Sprite Sisters played their best, along with the other sixteen young musicians.

Then there were a string quartet, the junior jazz band and some solo performances.

Pretty Myrna Shoemaker played a Chopin *Nocturne* on the piano; Lucy Chung and Lisha Olakimedji played an incredibly fast duet on their violins with great gusto. Milton Staples, an American boy whose father was said to be a diplomat, played a hauntingly lovely tune on the cornet.

Everything was going beautifully. There were now only two more performances before the interval: Verena Glass and the Sprite Sisters. After this, the senior school would perform.

Behind the stage curtains, the Sprite Sisters sat in a huddle, tense with excitement and worry. Ash and Ariel's 'accident', as everybody referred to it, had upset the four sisters.

They all knew who was responsible: Glenda Glass.

'She flipped us over on the stage just like that,' said Ash, still amazed at Glenda's power.

In a whisper, Flame reminded her sisters how they had to sit, and that they must arrange their chairs quickly and confidently, as if this was how they always played together.

'It will be really weird to play with my back to people,' said Ash.

'I know, Ash, I'm sorry, but it's better than having our act ruined,' said Flame.

'Yep, I know,' agreed Ash.

'What we must think about is creating the Circle of Power as we play,' said Flame. 'We can't hold hands this evening, so we have to *think* the connection between us in our minds – *feel* it. At the same time, we have to concentrate on playing well.'

Ariel looked baffled and made a face.

Marina looked anxious.

'Listen, think about the Circle of Power and I'm sure the playing will take care of itself,' said Flame. 'We know our three pieces back to front. We have practised them to perfection many, many times. Just *feel* the connection between us – the Sprite Sisters. Then we'll be fine.'

How do I know this? Flame thought, amazed at herself. Where did that idea come from?

The audience was clapping.

'Verena is next – then us,' said Ash, standing up.

'Good luck!' various girls called to Verena, as she stepped out between the curtains at the back of the stage.

Verena began the first of her two songs. She had a voice as clear as glass.

Flame peered through a crack in the curtains and scanned the audience. There was her friend Pia – and there was Quinn, with his family.

Her knees always buckled a little when she saw him:

she liked him so much that it hurt. He was watching Verena and smiling.

Verena's voice soared and floated.

Flame's heart sank.

Quinn may smile at me too, she thought. He smiles at everyone – and she *is* a wonderful singer.

Through the curtain, Flame noticed that Glenda Glass was sitting on an aisle seat, two rows behind Grandma. Luckily I will be able to keep an eye on her, she thought.

A few minutes later, Verena finished her second song to thunderous applause.

'Bravo! Well done!' people shouted.

The curtain opened. Verena walked through, her beautiful face flushed with excitement and success.

'Right!' said Flame. 'We're on!'

CHAPTER FOURTEEN

THE CIRCLE OF POWER

THE CURTAINS opened. The lights blazed.

'Ladies and Gentlemen, it is with great pleasure that I introduce to you the Sprite Sisters!' boomed Mr Taylor, through the microphone. Drysdale's School's head of music waved his right arm with an extravagant flourish towards the four girls.

Flame, Marina, Ash and Ariel Sprite stepped forward, smiled and bowed.

The audience clapped and clapped.

Someone – probably Dad – shouted, 'Hurrah!'

There they were, high up on the stage, underneath the

bright stage lights on their big night – the first time they had ever played together in public.

Flame had a slightly woozy feeling of déjà vu as she looked around at the wide brown stage. She looked out at the audience: five hundred people looked back.

Flame fixed Glenda in her sights and stood tall.

A moment later and the four Sprite Sisters had arranged their seats and music stands into a circle on the school stage. They sat down on their seats and started to tune their instruments. Flame sat facing the audience; Marina was to her left and Ariel to her right. And opposite, with her back to the audience, sat Ash.

On the front row, Batty Blenkinsop remarked to his wife, 'Odd way to sit.'

'Doesn't surprise me – the whole family is a bit odd,' muttered the Gargoyle. 'They had better not let down the school.'

'What *is* going on?' whispered Mum, confused. 'Why are they sitting like that? We can't see Ash – they've never played like this before.'

'I have no idea,' whispered Dad. 'Perhaps it's just another of the strange things that have happened this week. I'm beginning to wonder if my daughters are normal at all.'

Mum looked worried. 'I hope they are going to be okay.'

'They'll be fine, love,' he smiled.

Flame looked at her sisters. Their faces were flushed with

excitement. She tucked her violin under her chin and sat poised, ready to play.

Marina flexed her bow arm and looked out at the audience. Of all the Sprite Sisters, she was the one who most loved to perform.

Ash sat straight and leaned in towards her cello: she felt calm, as always.

Ariel tilted her head, ready to blow into her silver flute. Her heart was beating very quickly and her eyes looked like huge grey saucers. This is very different from playing at home in front of Mum, Dad and Grandma, she thought. I hope I don't forget anything.

Their practice had been perfect. The stage was set. The audience waited.

Out of the corner of her right eye, Grandma could just see Glenda: she had raised her chin and was staring straight at the Sprite Sisters.

Come on, girls, thought Grandma. Remember the Circle of Power.

In her mind, she threw a circle of light around her granddaughters.

Flame smiled at her sisters. 'We have played these pieces a hundred times,' she whispered. 'Are you ready?'

Marina, Ash and Ariel nodded.

Flame counted, 'One, two, three,' and off they went – beautifully, smoothly, perfectly in time.

* * *

Glenda Glass looked at the four sisters playing on stage and her heart grew colder. She turned her face slightly to look at Marilyn Sprite's still beautiful profile and her heart turned to white-hot fire. Over forty years – and this woman still made her stomach curdle with rage.

Well, now it is time to get my own back, she thought. I'll make the whole family suffer.

A grim smile flitted across her face as she turned back to look at the Sprite Sisters, who were now completely absorbed in their music.

Glenda Glass laid her right hand on her thigh and then raised it very, very slowly, as she folded her fingers inwards and extended her index finger. With the smallest of movements, she flexed her hand a little – right past Mum, two rows in front – until she was pointing directly at Ash's back.

Deep within her, she summoned her power.

Peeeyoww! Invisible darts of power shot out of Glenda's finger and hit Ash in the back, then flew sideways to Ariel and Marina – who missed their beats.

Ash jolted as if hit by a bullet. At the same time, a string broke on her cello. *Zchwweeeep*, it went as it lashed round, cutting her across the face and hand. Ash cried out, nearly dropped her cello – and they all stopped playing.

Damn, thought Glenda. I can't reach the eldest girl – she's being shielded by the one in front – but I've got the cellist and the others.

Marina and Ariel held their foreheads, as if nursing pounding headaches.

Flame stood up, blazing with anger, but had just enough self-control not to shout out at Glenda. Instead, she rushed over to Ash and supported her cello.

The judges sat up in their seats, concerned. Batty Blenkinsop and Mum stood up and walked quickly towards the stage. Various members of the audience stood up, wondering what was happening.

Ash was pale; blood trickled down her right cheek. She pulled a tissue out of her skirt pocket and dabbed her face, then stood up and smiled wanly at Flame.

'Hey ho,' she said. 'We tried.'

'We're not beaten yet!' said Flame. 'Come on, Mum has a spare string – we'll soon have your cello fixed.'

'Then what?' said Ash.

'Then we play on – only this time we think even more strongly about the Circle of Power! We weren't focusing on it properly – I don't think the Circle formed. We were concentrating so hard on playing perfectly.'

'Okay,' agreed Ash shakily, dabbing her face again.

Mum was running up the steps on to the stage holding her handbag, inside which were, indeed, complete sets of spare strings for all three stringed instruments.

The audience started chattering.

Mr Taylor bounded through the stage curtains and leaped to the front of the stage, clutching the microphone.

'Ladies and gentlemen, please would you bear with us for a few minutes,' he said. 'We have a small problem with a broken cello string. Mrs Sprite will soon have things fixed and the Sprite Sisters will resume their wonderful music.'

Not for long, thought Glenda, smoothing her sumptuous velvet shawl over her shoulders.

'Good Lord!' said Oswald Foffington-Plinker. 'Whatever is happening? That girl has blood on her face!'

'It seems the cello string broke,' replied Glenda, curling her mouth into a satisfied smile.

'And why are those other girls holding their heads?' he asked.

'Perhaps the Sprite Sisters are not up to a live performance,' said Glenda. 'Not like Verena.'

'Humph,' said Oswald, scratching his right ear. The Sprite Sisters had always seemed pretty confident to him.

Batty Blenkinsop was now on stage with the school nurse, who was checking Ash's cut face and hand.

The headmaster of Drysdale's hated any kind of public disruption – and this was the second time this week. Only three days ago, there'd been all that kerfuffle about Mrs Crump's floating spectacles and the last strands of his hair had fallen out, leaving him completely bald – and here he was again, with a row of judges, five hundred people watching him, an interrupted concert and a child with a bleeding face.

'Everything okay, Ottalie?' he asked.

'Yes, fine, Brian – we'll soon be ready.' Mum smiled her pretty smile – and Batty melted.

'You are so resourceful!' he said.

In a jiffy, Mum had attached the new string to the cello's tailpiece and was wrapping it around the peg at the top, whilst Ash held it steady over the bridge.

Flame beckoned Marina and Ariel to one side. They both looked a little wobbly.

'She hurt us!' whispered Ariel, close to tears.

'I know, pumpkin – we won't let her do it again,' Flame stroked her little sister's soft hair back from her face.

'Are you okay, Marina?' she asked softly.

'Yep, think so,' replied Marina, rubbing her forehead. 'It felt like she'd stunned us or something.'

'Her power is very strong,' whispered Flame. 'We *must* focus on the Circle of Power. We were playing well, but we weren't connecting with our power. Glenda will hurt us again if we don't protect ourselves. Do you understand?'

'It's not easy to think of two things at once,' said Marina.

'We must *not* let this evil woman beat us!' hissed Flame. 'Come on! Think about the Circle of Power – if we really *feel* it, we'll be protected. Do you remember how we felt, when we sat on the bed and held hands?'

Marina and Ariel nodded.

'Well, hold *that* feeling in your mind as you play,' said Flame. 'It will probably make our music even better.'

'That's a good thought,' said Marina.

'Resolve!' whispered Flame to her sisters.

'Resolve,' they agreed.

Mum had now fixed the string and waited as her daughters sat down and tuned, once again, to the note 'A'.

Batty and the nurse left the stage. Mr Taylor hovered in the wings.

'Well done, girls,' said Mum. 'Start the piece again and you'll be fine.'

She smiled at her daughters – and they smiled back at her.

'Thanks, Mum,' said Flame.

'How's your face feeling?' Mum asked Ash.

'It's fine now, thanks, Mum,' she replied, drawing the horsehair bow over the cello strings and adjusting the pegs one last time.

'Flame?' whispered Mum.

'Yes?'

'Why are you sitting like this?'

'We agreed it felt better,' whispered Flame, smiling.

'Oh – okay. Well, good luck!' Baffled, Mum returned to her seat.

The audience settled down.

'Okay,' said Flame very softly, looking at each of her sisters. 'The Circle of Power!'

'The Circle of Power!' they whispered.

'East, south, west and north. Our powers are balanced,' said Flame, under her breath.

For a few seconds, the Sprite Sisters sat still and silent.

'Can you feel the power?' whispered Flame.

Her sisters nodded.

'My arms are tingling,' Ariel giggled.

They all smiled as they felt their magic power course through their arms and hands. The blue light blazed round them.

'Hold the Circle of Power,' said Flame.

The audience was silent: you could have heard a pin drop.

A few people thought they could see a small flicker of blue light around the Sprite Sisters – but no one was quite sure.

In her seat, Grandma could see the blue light getting stronger. They are gaining their power, she thought. Well done, girls – keep going!

In her seat two rows behind, Glenda Glass moved her right hand ever so gently and pointed her finger once again. She, too, could see the glowing blue light around the sisters – and knew exactly what they were doing.

Hmm, thought Glenda, they are getting pretty good, these girls. Better send them something really unpleasant.

And as Glenda Glass laughed a silent laugh, off the Sprite Sisters went again. For a second, Glenda listened as their music soared. She saw that the audience was entranced.

And she saw that, as the Sprite Sisters played, the Circle of Power grew stronger and stronger, until it became a huge force. The four girls played as they had never played before. It was as if their music had been touched by magic.

Right. Bye, bye Sprite Sisters, growled Glenda to herself, sending arrows and darts and bullets of power through her fingers.

But none of her missiles had any effect. Instead of hurting the Sprite Sisters, Glenda saw her dark power bounce off their Circle of Power – and hurtle back to her.

'Argh!' she winced, grabbing her neck as a dart of pain hit her.

Oswald turned. 'What's the matter, Glenda?'

'*Nothing!*' she snarled through gritted teeth – and hurled another avalanche of power towards the Sprite Sisters.

Ferrrrwroooomm! Shwiiiiiieyyy! Zzzzzzzweeeee! – it went.

But to no avail: the more power Glenda threw at them, the harder it bounced off their Circle of Power – and came right back to her. It was if she was shooting at bullet-proof glass – and none of this, she realised, was exposing the Sprite Sisters' power.

Together, their power is stronger than mine, she thought. And she clenched her fists tight.

No! No! No! thought Glenda. You will not win this one.

As the girls' music soared to its finale, Glenda Glass sent one more bolt of magic at the Sprite Sisters. It was one bolt too many.

'Eeerrrrh!' She gave a strangled scream, clutched her stomach and left leg, and tried to stand up. Glenda Glass was in agony – wounded by her own dark power.

'Get me out of here!' she cried, seething in anger, as the Sprite Sisters held their final note and the audience burst into applause.

'Wonderful! Marvellous! Bravo! Terrific performance!' people shouted as Batty Blenkinsop jumped out of his seat and rushed around to the centre aisle.

Clapping hard, the astonished audience watched as Batty and Oswald Foffington-Plinker each placed an arm under Glenda Glass's and carried her out of the school hall. Behind them, Gloria teetered on her high heels.

Through a small crack in the stage curtain, Verena Glass watched her family leave the concert hall. Everybody leaves me, she thought, and snapped the curtain shut.

In her seat, Grandma put her head in her hand and whispered, 'Thank goodness for that.' She wiped away a tear from her face and thought, They did it! That'll teach Glenda Glass!

Dad squeezed Mum's hand and smiled at her. 'Well done, love,' he said.

Tears trickled down Mum's face as her daughters took their bow. Dad and Grandma smiled at one another.

'Phew!' said Dad, rubbing his chin.

'Yes – phew!' laughed Grandma, dabbing her eyes.

On the stage, the four Sprite Sisters listened to the loud applause – and they smiled.

'We did it!' said Marina. 'We beat her – and we played

really well! How amazing is that!'

'Yep, we did it!' laughed Flame.

'Batty and Oswald had to carry Glenda out!' giggled Ariel.

'That was really funny!' laughed Ash.

Flame smiled at Ash and touched her arm. 'Thank you, sis,' she said. 'You were injured but you carried on. We couldn't have done it without you!'

Ash smiled her quiet smile.

'How do you feel, pumpkin?' Flame turned to Ariel.

'Fab-fantastic!' giggled the smallest Sprite Sister.

Flame looked out at the sea of faces and saw Quinn, smiling and clapping his hands as hard as he could – and her heart skipped a beat.

Then, clutching their instruments, the Sprite Sisters made their way off the stage to join their family. The audience got up for the coffee break.

Verena Glass walked past the Sprite family as they hugged each other, all smiling happily.

'Verena!' called Mum, spotting her.

Verena turned and walked towards her.

'You sang absolutely beautifully, dear!' said Mum. 'You have such a talent!'

'Thank you, Mrs Sprite!' smiled Verena. 'Do you know what happened to my family?'

'It seems your grandmother was taken ill,' said Mum.

'Is she all right?' asked Verena, anxious.

'I'm sure she will be,' said Mum. 'I believe your uncle has taken her home. We'll take you back, dear, so don't worry. I'll get Colin to ring and let them know.'

'Thank you!' Verena looked hugely relieved. 'I thought they'd forgotten me!'

A few metres away, in the hubbub of the hall, Quinn came up to Flame.

'You were amazing!' he said.

'Was I? Thank you!'

'You sure were!' he smiled. 'Your eyes were blazing – like you were on a crusade or something!'

'Oh! Well – I was, in a way,' said Flame. 'I'm glad you could come.'

'There's never a dull moment around you and your sisters,' said Quinn. 'Come on – let's get a juice.'

CHAPTER FIFTEEN

✸

AFTER THE CONCERT

✸ ✸

✸

THE SECOND half of the concert passed in the way in which concerts usually pass. The senior school played and sang, every one of them facing the audience. People clapped. All the strings stayed intact. Nobody hurled dark powers at anyone else or got carried out. No one spotted the smallest flickering of blue light. Everything went swimmingly – the judges looked impressed and even Batty Blenkinsop started to relax and enjoy himself.

The Sprite Sisters sat with their parents. At Mum's invitation, Verena joined them and sat next to Marina. After the concert, they got into the two Sprite cars and drove home, first stopping to drop off Verena. Flame had swapped with Grandma and drove home with Dad, to avoid being near Verena.

In the big kitchen of Sprite Towers, the family drank mugs of thick, dark cocoa and ate cheesy toast. Everyone was hungry.

For the first ten minutes, Mum talked about the girls' performance and how well they had played. She wanted to go through each piece.

'I still don't quite understand why you sat like that, girls – in that circle?' she asked, clutching her mug of cocoa.

The Sprite Sisters looked at one another.

'Er, we decided we'd like to face each other – and Ash said she didn't mind not seeing anyone,' said Flame, quickly. 'Isn't that right, Ash?'

'Yep,' agreed Ash, scooping up a piece of melted cheese.

'You've never done that before – why tonight?' said Mum. 'It looked a bit odd. I wondered what you were doing.'

The Sprite Sisters were unusually quiet and seemed very focused on eating their toast.

When none of them responded, Mum said, 'More cocoa anyone?'

'What an unpleasant woman Verena's grandmother is – what's her name – Glenda,' said Dad, changing the subject. 'Had a handshake like a dead fish and seemed as cold as one, too.'

They all laughed.

'I didn't realise you two knew each other, Mother,' he said to Grandma.

'We danced together in the same ballet company,' she replied. 'She was very jealous of me, as I got chosen for the star roles. I was the better dancer and she could not accept it. Then, she was very put out when your father and I fell in love. It seems she has never forgiven me.'

'Ah! So she was keen on Pa – but he liked you?' asked Dad, grinning.

'Exactly,' said Grandma.

'Blimey, you'd have thought she'd have got over it by now – she's had four husbands!' said Dad.

'Yes, you would – but she's a strange woman,' smiled Grandma.

'And you say she is a Sprite?' said Mum.

'Her grandmother was Margaret, Sidney Sprite's sister,' explained Grandma.

'Oh, so you're cousins – like you and Sheldon?' said Mum. 'How extraordinary! What a small world, eh?

'I heard Oswald Foffington-Plinker having a go at you again about selling the house, Colin,' continued Mum.

A look of intense gloom spread over Dad's face – and Mum wished she hadn't mentioned the subject at all.

'Hmm,' he said, reaching for a second bit of cheesy toast. 'Oswald doesn't take "no" for an answer – and bills at Sprite Towers don't get any smaller. He seemed to know exactly what the roof needed spent on it, which was a bit uncanny.'

Mum did not want to spoil the mood of the evening.

'It's getting late, but I just want to say that I am very proud of you all, girls,' she said. 'You have worked so hard and we have had a wonderful evening – so, well done!'

'Hear, hear,' agreed Dad.

'Yes, well done!' smiled Grandma.

'Do you think Drysdale's will win the competition and that we will play in London?' asked Ariel.

'That would be terrific, but even if you *don't* win, you should still all be proud of your performance,' said Mum.

'When will we know?' asked Ash.

'In a few days,' replied Mum.

'And we can still go to London for the weekend, even if you don't win,' said Dad.

'Cool!' said Marina.

'Thank you, Mum, for all your help,' said Flame. 'We couldn't have done it without you.'

'Yes, and thanks for the string rescue,' said Ash.

'You are most welcome,' said Mum, bowing her head.

'To Mum!' said Marina, holding up her cocoa mug. 'Here's a cocoa mug toast!'

And the Sprite family clacked their mugs together across the table.

'To Mum!' they shouted.

Half an hour later, Ariel, Flame, Marina and Ash raced up to bed.

'Night, Sidney!' they shouted, as they passed their great-great-grandfather's portrait at the bottom of the wide mahogany staircase.

Ariel stopped to tell Sidney Sprite that they'd seen off Glenda Glass at the concert.

Grandma, who was heading upstairs herself, watched as she talked to the portrait.

Ariel giggled and then turned to hold Grandma's hand. 'He says he's very pleased,' she said, as they walked up the staircase.

'I am sure he is!' laughed Grandma. It was no surprise to her that Ariel communicated with her great-great-grandfather, even though he had been dead for fifty-five years and despite the fact that no one else could hear him talking back.

This house is full of magic, she thought. I expect we will feel it more, now that all the girls have their power.

'I'll tell them a quick story,' said Grandma to Mum on the landing. Mum had been gathering up the girls' dresses and socks in a large wicker laundry basket which she now held under her arm.

'Okey-doke. I'll go down and help Colin get cleared up,' said Mum. She kissed each of her daughters and returned to the kitchen.

'Let's sit on your bed tonight, Ash,' suggested Grandma. They trooped up the corridor to Ash's room, which was neat and tidy and painted a pretty shade of green. On the windowsill were pots full of plants and seedlings.

The sisters sat on the pale blue bed cover in their dressing gowns. Grandma sat at the end of the bed, so she could see them all.

'What an evening, eh?' she smiled. 'Glenda Glass hurt by her own power and you four all in one piece and stars of the show. You did incredibly well, all of you. That was quite a feat you pulled off. She sent you some horrible dark power – and you resisted it. Do you now see what an evil woman Glenda is, and what a desire for vengeance she still holds? She won't forget this defeat – but now you have your magic powers to protect you.'

For a few seconds there was silence as the Sprite Sisters took on board the fact that they had a real enemy and that she would be back.

'Were you frightened as you sat in the circle?' asked Grandma. 'How did it feel when she sent her magic power?'

'I thought my head would explode,' said Ariel. 'I felt all wibbly wobbly.'

'I was frightened, Grandma,' said Marina. 'I felt dizzy and had a horrible headache, like Ariel. It was really diffi-cult trying to play the music and think about our power and Glenda, all at the same time – and with all those people watching us.'

'Yes, that was tricky,' agreed Flame.

'Well, you did very well,' said Grandma.

'How did it feel sitting with your back to the audience, Ash?' asked Grandma.

'I didn't mind not seeing people, but I felt vulnerable not being able to see Glenda,' said Ash. 'Funny feeling when you think someone behind you will hurt you and you can't see it coming.'

'You took the full force of her anger – and shielded me,' Flame said to Ash.

'Grandma, will she try to hurt us again?' piped up Ariel.

'It's possible, love – but you'll know what to expect next time,' said Grandma. 'Now you all have your magic powers, lots of things may happen.'

'Like what?' asked Marina.

'You will find you are able to see and feel things other people cannot see,' explained Grandma. 'You know the way insects see things differently to humans – and eagles can see a mile away in sharp focus? Well, it's a bit like that.

'You girls must always remember that if you work together you will be balanced – and that is the greatest power of all,' continued Grandma. 'When you bring your elements of fire, water, earth and air together – east, south, west and north – then you can create powerful magic. You learned how to use your power wisely this evening – and I am very proud of you all,'

Grandma looked at Flame. 'You look as if you have something on your mind.'

'I was wondering how strong Glenda's power is compared to ours,' said Flame. 'I have a feeling that, at the moment, if all four of us are together, then we are stronger; but if there are only three of us, she's probably stronger.'

Grandma considered this. 'If that's what feels right to you, then that is probably true,' she said.

Flame looked at her grandmother's face. 'Yes,' she agreed.

'Always go by what you *feel*, as well as what you think,' said Grandma. 'Use your mind to think around a problem, analyse and understand it. Then make the decision from your heart. That way, you will make the right one.'

Grandma looked at her granddaughters and could see they were listening hard.

'Remember that you succeeded this evening because you used your powers to defend yourselves – not to set out to hurt anyone – and because you kept them secret. I don't expect anyone but us and Glenda knew what was really happening.

'You sisters are all growing in strength. Glenda's power is unlikely to get any stronger. At the moment you need each other to balance your power. Eventually you will find that balance alone.'

Grandma smiled at her granddaughters. They all nodded.

'Grandma, will you tell us about Sidney Sprite's magic powers?' asked Ariel.

Flame, Marina and Ash smiled.

'Your great-great-grandfather was a wonderful and clever man and he had powerful magic,' smiled Grandma. 'One day I will tell you about him – but, now, my darlings, it is time for bed.'

CHAPTER SIXTEEN

SATURDAY AT SPRITE TOWERS

It was Saturday morning. The birds were singing and the sky was blue. The sun shone down on Sprite Towers and the big house hummed with activity.

Dad was mowing the huge lawns on his ride-on mower. Mum was weeding the rose garden by the side of the terrace. Flame and Ash were picking strawberries in the vegetable garden. Marina was cleaning out the guinea pig and rabbit hutches at the bottom of the garden. Ariel was cleaning out the gerbil and hamster cages in the utility room, with the door kept tightly shut. Grandma was baking in the kitchen.

Only the animals were doing nothing: Bert was snoring

in his basket in the kitchen (he didn't like Dad's lawn mower) and Pudding lay curled up on the Windsor chair.

'I've had an idea,' said Flame to Ash, as she put a handful of strawberries into a bowl.

A few minutes later, the two sisters ran to find Marina; then all three ran to find their father. A minute after that, they burst into the kitchen.

Grandma looked up. 'Where's Mum?' they asked.

'Here,' said Mum, walking in behind them, holding a bunch of roses.

'Mum, it's such a nice day, could we have some friends over to play rounders this afternoon?' asked Flame.

'Please, please!' said Marina, jumping up and down.

Mum looked at Grandma, who said, 'It's okay by me, dear.'

'Have you asked your father?' said Mum.

'He says it's fine by him and to ask you,' said Flame. 'Please, Mum, it'll be such fun!'

'Okay – but not hundreds of people,' said Mum. 'It's only a week since we had your party, remember!'

'Nine a side?' said Flame.

'Okay,' agreed Mum.

Ariel came out of the utility room.

'Mum and Dad say we can have a rounders match this afternoon!' said Marina.

'Fab-fantastic!' said Ariel.

Grandma smiled at Mum. 'I think I'd better make another

batch of scones and two more chocolate cakes,' she said.

Mum laughed. 'It never stops here, does it?'

There was much debate about who to invite: each of the Sprite Sisters wanted several friends. The girls at Drysdale's all played rounders but the boys played cricket and were good bowlers and fielders, so they enjoyed the Sprites' rounders matches, too.

Within half an hour, the Sprite Sisters had agreed their list and the friends were phoned and invited.

Mum asked Ash to go and ask Dad to invite Batty Blenkinsop, so he could referee the match. Dad saw Ash approaching and stopped the lawn mower. He got out his mobile and called Batty, who said he would be delighted to come.

'And Ottalie says to ask Virginia if she'd like to join us for tea,' said Dad.

Ash made a face at him. 'Not the Gargoyle, Dad!' she whispered.

'I'm sure she'd be very pleased,' replied Batty.

'Right – well, see you later,' said Dad into his mobile, smiling at Ash.

'Must we have the Gargoyle here?' she asked.

'Bit difficult not to, love,' he grinned, but she knew he agreed with her really.

Ash and Dad laid out the rounders pitch with four heavy metal bases and wooden posts. Dad marked out the bowling and batting squares with the white-line machine he used for the tennis court, then they went to pick more strawberries for tea.

Flame and Ariel went up to the attics to find the rounders bats and balls, took these down to the garden, then prepared trays of glasses and jugs for the lemonade. Marina and Mum made sandwiches.

Then everyone helped to carry chairs and tables down the garden to the edge of the big lawn. Tablecloths were spread over the tables and rugs laid out on the grass.

At two o'clock, everything was ready. The Sprite Sisters' friends gathered in the garden at Sprite Towers, wearing shorts, T-shirts and trainers.

When Quinn and his sister Janey arrived however, Verena Glass was with them.

'I hope you won't mind – we've brought Verena,' said Quinn, smiling. 'Janey and I stopped in town with Mum on the way here and we bumped into Verena and her uncle. I suggested she come with us to Sprite Towers – thought you wouldn't mind.'

Verena smiled thinly and held out a letter she was carrying.

'Uncle Oswald was about to post this to your father – but since I was coming here with Janey and Quinn, he asked me to bring it instead,' she said, flicking back her long blond hair.

Flame knew exactly what this letter was about:

Oswald's offer for Sprite Towers.

'I'm not giving that to Dad now – it can wait!' exploded Flame, grabbing the letter from Verena's hand. 'I'll go and put it in the house.'

'What's the matter?' asked Mum, as Flame burst into the kitchen and threw the letter on the table. 'Why are you crying? What's happened?'

'Verena's come with Quinn – and she's brought this! It's from her uncle!' shouted Flame.

'Oh dear,' said Mum.

Flame stood by the table, feeling as if her world was crashing down around her.

'Why does he like Verena, Mum? She's horrible!' she said.

Mum put her arm around her daughter's shoulder and drew her close.

'*You* like her too!' said Flame. 'You had her with us at the concert and even brought her back in car afterwards!'

'Yes – because that was the kind thing to do,' said Mum. 'We couldn't leave Verena on her own, Flame. Her family had to take her grandmother home, remember.'

'You wouldn't believe what a cow she is to me at school!' sobbed Flame. 'I can't believe Quinn is friends with her! She's only doing it to get at me! I wish you knew what she was really like!'

'I know exactly what Verena is like,' said Mum. 'I know she is cold and manipulative – but I also see that she is very lonely underneath.'

'So?' said Flame.

'So, show her some compassion,' said Mum.

'There's not a kind bone in her body, Mum!' said Flame. 'She's always being mean to us!'

'Her kindness is in there somewhere, love,' said Mum. 'It's just buried a bit more deeply than in most people. And that's no reason why *you* shouldn't be kind to *her*.'

Flame sighed. Mum hugged her tight.

'Now, dry your eyes and go and look after your guests,' said Mum. 'Don't let this spoil your afternoon.'

Flame walked over the lawn. Marina ran up to her.

'Are you okay?' she asked, putting her hand on her sister's shoulder.

'Yep,' nodded Flame.

'Come on, we're going to have a great afternoon!' smiled Marina. 'Don't think about Verena; think about the rounders match.'

It did not take long for Flame to relax. She loved playing sport: when a game had started, she forgot about everything else.

Down on the huge rolling lawn, Grandma and the Gargoyle sat on wicker armchairs under the big copper beech tree.

The players gathered around Batty Blenkinsop. Dressed in whites and wearing a Panama hat, he nominated Flame and Quinn as captains and bowlers and asked them to choose their teams.

After some debate, the teams were agreed. Mum and Dad were to play on opposing sides. Verena was reluctant to join in, but Mum insisted. Flame and Quinn wrote out a list of the two sides on a big sheet of white paper and pinned it to an easel that Dad had found in one of the sheds.

'This all looks very professional,' said Batty and tossed a coin.

'Heads,' said Flame – and heads it was. 'Okay, my team bats first,' she said.

Quinn's team took up their positions in the field.

Flame's team lined up behind the pitch. As bowler, Flame batted first: she gave the ball an almighty whack, scored the first rounder and the game got off to a roaring start.

For the next hour, as the sun burned down on the grass, the players ran and jumped; they threw balls and they caught them. They batted and they dived to touch the bases.

Hearts thumped, muscles stretched and sweat trickled down faces as the batting team tried to make their rounders and the fielding team tried to stop them.

Batty Blenkinsop watched them all like a hawk.

At half-time, Quinn's team came into bat and Flame's team took up their fielding positions.

An hour later, after a spectacular catch by Pia's brother, Vivek, way out in the deeps, Quinn's team were all out. The match was over.

'Fantastic play!' everyone said, as they gathered around Batty Blenkinsop.

'Very impressive game – well played, all of you!' said Batty.

'That was really good fun!' Dad said to Mum. He put his arm around her shoulders and kissed her on the cheek.

'Quiet for the scores, please!' announced Batty, holding up his arm. 'The final scores are: Flame's team: nineteen rounders; Quinn's team: eighteen and a half rounders. That means the winners of the Sprite Towers Rounders Match are Flame's team!'

Everybody clapped.

'Three cheers for Quinn's team for giving us such a good game!' shouted Flame. 'Hip, hip, hooray!'

Her team cheered. Quinn smiled.

'And three cheers to Mr Blenkinsop for being a sterling referee!' shouted Dad.

'Hip, hip, hooray!' they all went again.

Then everyone made their way to the beech tree, under which was a tea to gladden the heart and stomach of any tired player.

Spread out on the tables were freshly-made scones bursting with homemade jam; home-grown strawberries and a jug of thick cream; huge piles of sandwiches; gooey chocolate cakes with thick fudgy icing; fairy cakes covered with vanilla crunch and big jugs of iced elderflower cordial and homemade lemonade.

The Sprite Sisters and their friends sat on the rugs with plates piled high with food, munching and chatting happily.

'This is heavenly!' said Su-Ling, licking her lips.

'Yum!' said Alex Tolver, his mouth full of strawberries.

'What a wonderful afternoon!' said Quinn, smiling at Flame.

The grown-ups sat on the big wicker chairs and drank cups of tea.

Verena Glass sat on the ground, close to Mum's chair.

'Did you know that the game of rounders was documented as early as the seventeenth century?' said Batty, lifting a large piece of chocolate cake to his mouth.

'Really?' said Mum.

Batty looked delirious as he bit into the cake. 'Wonderful!' he said, chewing happily. 'The way you and Marilyn rustle up all this lovely food for people is quite amazing.'

'Thank you, Brian,' Mum smiled.

The Gargoyle shot her husband a withering look. She was a dreadful cook and was deeply envious of the Sprites' food. She loved being invited to tea, but it irked her to see her husband enjoying himself so much.

'Yes, delicious – thank you,' she said to Mum, through gritted teeth.

'You're very welcome,' smiled Mum.

'Any news on the music competition yet, Brian?' asked Dad.

'I expect to hear on Monday morning,' replied Batty. 'Fingers crossed for Drysdale's, eh?'

* * *

Batty and the Gargoyle went home after tea. The Sprite Sisters and their friends helped carry the plates and glasses back to the house, then sat on the grass and talked.

Mum and Grandma were loading the dishwasher, when Dad walked into the kitchen carrying a tray of plates and bowls.

'What's this?' he said, seeing a letter addressed to him propped up on the table.

'Verena brought it,' said Mum.

'Oh Lord, I expect it's from Oswald flipping Pompington-doodah,' said Dad, putting the tray down.

He sighed heavily, tore the envelope and pulled out the letter. Mum and Grandma read it over his shoulders.

'He wants to talk to us formally about buying Sprite Towers,' said Dad, his jaw muscles tightening. 'Persistent chap.'

Mum took his arm and squeezed it. He smiled down at her.

'Sprite Towers is not for sale,' said Dad. 'I don't know how we will afford to stay here for much longer *and* keep the girls at Drysdale's, but we'll do whatever it takes to keep this house. This is our home. This is where we belong.'

Grandma walked out of the kitchen door and down the garden. In the middle of the lawn she stopped, turned, and looked back at the house. Sidney Sprite's two towers were glinting in the sunshine.

She listened to the sound of laughter filling the garden

and she thought how much she and her family loved Sprite Towers.

I know who is behind this, thought Grandma – and once again felt a chill go through her. It's Glenda Glass, she thought. It's Glenda who wants to take our home away – and she is using Oswald to get it.

This could be the start of a big fight, she thought, looking up at the sky.

Then Grandma's spirit grew once more. The girls have their powers, she thought. They are getting stronger. We will find a way to protect Sprite Towers.

Meanwhile, down on the lawn, Flame was talking with Quinn and a small group of friends, on the rugs.

Verena stood up and started to walk towards the house. Much as she wanted Quinn's attention, she did not want to stay sitting near Flame.

She was looking down at the grass as she walked, when someone touched her on the arm. It was Marina.

'Come and have a look at our animals!' she said.

Verena knew that Marina was trying to give Flame some time with Quinn, but nevertheless she appreciated the distraction.

'Okay,' she agreed.

Flame looked up and saw the two girls walking away and she smiled at Quinn.

Ash ran to join Marina and Verena, as they made their

way to the bottom of the garden.

Marina and Ash got out a variety of rabbits and guinea pigs, which they gave to Verena to hold.

'I have never had any animals,' she said, stroking a soft rabbit nose.

Then Marina said, 'Did you know that we are distant cousins?'

Verena screwed up her face.

'Cousins?' she said. 'Don't be silly!'

'*Distant* cousins,' said Marina. 'Your great-great-grandmother was the sister of Sidney Sprite, our great-great-grandfather. Dad told us the other day.'

'That makes us distant cousins,' added Ash.

Verena did not know what to say. She felt confused. Part of her wanted to make a sarky remark about the Sprites – and the other part of her felt empty and sad.

'So, you mean we are related?' she said.

Marina and Ash nodded.

'Like family?'

Marina and Ash nodded again. Ash took the rabbit Verena was holding. Verena did not notice.

She moved away, sat down on an old iron roller that was propped up against the stables wall and stared silently at the ground. She wanted to trust these girls – her new, distant cousins – but she did not know how.

Verena Glass had learned never to trust anyone. The only person she felt vaguely safe with was the mother of these girls – these sisters, who protected each other fiercely, as everyone at Drysdale's knew.

Marina and Ash looked at one another: they were not expecting a still, silent Verena, staring at the ground.

Just then Ariel came bouncing towards them, waving her arms.

'Come on!' she shouted. 'Everyone's going! She saw Verena. 'What's the matter? What's happened?'

'We just told Verena she has Sprite blood running through her veins,' said Marina. 'She's bit surprised.'

'Isn't it weird?' giggled Ariel.

'Yes, weird is about it,' said Verena.

'Come on – let's get back!' said Ariel. 'Race you!' Immediately Marina and Ash started to run.

Verena stood up and watched the three sisters: they stopped, looked back at her and beckoned – but she stayed where she was. She wanted to run – to join in – but she could not.

For the first time in her life, Verena Glass found something impossible.

Later, when she was back at The Oaks, watching television with her grandmother, Verena thought about this moment.

She looked round at her grandmother, sitting at the far side of the sofa, and announced, 'The Sprite Sisters told me I am related to them.'

'Yes,' replied Glenda Glass, without moving. Verena

206

stared at her grandmother's profile.

'You mean you *knew*?'

Glenda turned to look at her granddaughter.

'Yes, of course: I am a Sprite,' she said. 'Your great-great grandmother was Sidney Sprite's sister, Margaret. The girls' grandmother, Marilyn Sprite, and I danced together in the ballet when we were younger. I know all about the Sprite family.'

'Why didn't you tell me?' asked Verena.

Her grandmother shrugged and turned back to the television. She was still seething with anger at her defeat by the Sprite Sisters at the school concert. Parts of her body still ached. Her mind was more focused than ever on revenge.

'Why hasn't anyone ever told me this?' Verena said again.

'Well, you know now,' said Glenda.

Verena got up to turn on the lamps in the darkening room. She felt restless, uneasy.

'What was in that letter Uncle Oswald gave me?' she asked, turning towards Glenda. 'Flame was very upset about it.'

'Yes, I expect she was.' Her grandmother gave a satisfied smile.

'Well, what was it?' asked Verena.

'Your uncle wants to buy Sprite Towers, turn it into a boutique hotel and build lots of houses on the grounds,' said Glenda. 'It was an offer to discuss selling the house for a lot of money.'

'But the Sprites live there!' said Verena.

'They do at the moment,' said Glenda, fixing her grand-daughter with a malicious eye. 'How would *you* like to live there, Verena?'

'Me? Don't be silly!' said Verena.

'I am never silly,' replied her grandmother. 'I ask again: how would you like to live there?'

'Where would the Sprites go?' asked Verena.

'Oh, they'll find somewhere else to live,' said Glenda. 'You have not answered my question.'

'I don't know,' said Verena.

'Well, think about it,' said Glenda. 'Oswald does not realise it, but I plan to have the Sprites out of that house and our family living there, soon. And I expect you, my granddaughter, to help me execute that plan. You can be my spy – my eye on the Sprites.'

Verena Glass said nothing. She saw the gleam of obsession in her grandmother's eyes – and she was frightened.

She walked out of the sitting room and climbed the dark stairs to her bedroom.

Her grandmother, she had realised this last week, was a cold woman who hardly seemed to notice her – except when she wanted her to do something. Now she had discovered her to be ruthless as well.

Who could she talk to? she wondered.

Her mother was thousands of miles away and her father had, once again, been unable to return home that weekend.

Verena had never felt so alone.

As Verena drew her bedroom curtains and turned on the lamp, the Sprite Sisters were pounding up the wide mahogany staircase at Sprite Towers and wearing out the stair carpet still further.

Half an hour later, with the girls settled in bed, Dad bolted the front door and sat down on the sofa, close to Mum. Bert sat on Grandma's lap as the three of them watched a film.

'Lovely day we've had!' said Dad, when the film had finished.

'Yes!' agreed Mum.

'It was wonderful, dears – we are very lucky,' said Grandma. 'I think I'll go up now.'

She placed Bert on the ground, then kissed her son and daughter-in-law goodnight.

'Goodnight, sleep well,' said Mum and Dad. 'And thank you for all your help today.'

Bert nestled by Mum's feet.

As Grandma walked through the hallway, she paused to look at the portrait of Sidney Sprite on the wall.

'Goodnight, Sidney; keep us safe,' she said, and she climbed the wide mahogany stairs to her bedroom.

On the second floor of the big house, the Sprite Sisters lay in their beds, relaxed and ready for sleep.

Flame Sprite started to think about her magic powers and Glenda, but she stopped and thought about Quinn, instead.

Marina was thinking about the rounders match, and what fun it had been.

Ash lay in bed and wondered if the monster slugs were happy in their new laboratory home.

Ariel Sprite yawned and felt her pink stubby fingers.

I am nine years and one week old, she thought. I am a Sprite Sister and I have magic powers – but I have to try to remember to use them responsibly.

Ariel yawned again. That might be difficult, she thought.

The timbers of the old house creaked as they settled in the damp night air.

Then, as if by magic, an air of stillness came over Sprite Towers.

The four Sprite Sisters curled up in their beds and fell into deep, dreamy sleep.

SPECIAL THANKS

With huge thanks to Brenda Gardner for her vision, to Anne Clark for her fine editing and all the Piccadilly Press team for their enthusiasm and hard work. Also to Chris Winn for bringing the Sprite world to life in his drawing, and to Simon Davis and Anna Gould for the super cover.

Thank you to all my wonderful friends and family. Especial thanks to my son, Alex and my daughter, Rosie; to Charlotte & Henry Crawley, Elisabeth & David Hawkey, Peter & Maria Edwards, Debbie Shannon & Steve Lepper, Preetie and Tushar Raja, Cathie and Dennis Bailey, Diana Alston, David Brittain, Geoff Davidson, Liz Hollis, Ian Nettleton, Diana Bylett and Caroline Holland, Mark Aylett and Corinne Livingstone for their kind and unstinting support.

And thank you to my young readers, Charlotte Houldey and Marina Ebbage –
the Sprite Sisters' first fans.